MW01124609

# Gold Hunters: Lure of the Superstitions

by

Lorenzo Rendon

**INGOT PUBLISHING™**

Alaska, USA

ISBN-13: 978-1540853158
ISBN-10: 1540853152



FIRST EDITION
INGOT PUBLISHING™

Cover design by Rocky Berlier

Book design and layout by Rocky Berlier
www.concierge-publishing.com

Manufactured in the United States of America

# DEDICATION

*This is for the ancestors. And their innocent voices that can still be heard, by those who dare to listen.*

# Acknowledgements

Thanks to my friends James and Shawna. James for our enduring friendship and his willingness to join me on some of my adventures. To Shawna, who joined me too, and her loyalty and constant encouragement. And to Anastasia, the love of my life, for always believing in me.

I owe a special thanks to Cynthia and Rocky. I learned so much from both of them. Rocky, my publisher, did amazing detail work. He did such a wonderful job of capturing the feel of the book in the cover artwork, and the petroglyphs. And to my editor Cynthia, for giving me the push I needed to make me better. Her knowledge of the business is immense. And her critiques for a new author were invaluable. I will be forever indebted to her for "showing me the ropes."

# FOREWORD

## This Story had to be Told!

Authors are often instructed to write what they know. In Gold Hunters: Lure of the Superstitions, Lorenzo Rendon did a superb job of weaving his many skills and experiences, along with such believable characters, that I could not put it down. That is until I was nearly finished, and then I slowed down to savor every word, because I didn't want the story to end.

There is something for every reader in this adventure: treasure hunting, danger, love, friendship, cultural and historical awareness, corruption, and a great deal of fun!

I was introduced to Lorenzo by a mutual friend. This began the hours of lively discussions—both on the phone and in person—over coffee, a meal, or a glass of wine, whenever he was in town.

At our first meeting, over iced tea (once I had met the "we can trust her" vetting), a large folder was pushed across the table to me, and all voices were lowered. I was then told a true story of a treasure hunt, which the author and our mutual friend had attempted.

In the folder were maps, diagrams, photographs, and notes. I have no sense of direction, and am practically dyslexic when it comes to map reading, but I understood the importance and value of these items. Add to this, both of the people sitting across the table from me have some Native American blood in their lineages, and are conscious, spiritual, ethical, and people of integrity. I left our meeting three hours later, knowing that this was going to be a fascinating project to coach the author through, and I looked forward to editing the first draft of the manuscript.

This story had to be told! Not only would it entertain readers, but it would also—in a non-preachy way—*inform* readers as a beneficial side effect! This is fiction, to be sure. However, just as many other authors have done (and done well), there is much truth, history, with many facts woven in.

Lorenzo was passionate about writing this story. When he presented his first draft, he included some research. He wondered whether it should be included as an addendum at the end of the book. I encouraged him to incorporate these facts into the body of the story as it would engage the readers more. The thought of having to recraft his manuscript to incorporate the research was daunting to him; he had already spent so much time on this project. I offered to help since I am a ghostwriter among other writer services, but he quickly rallied to the challenge and said, "No, let me take a stab at it." I admire him so much for that.

A few months later I heard back from Lorenzo with a heads-up that he was sending the integrated manuscript back to me. I was absolutely delighted at how he had resolved the issue. The results, I believe, will delight you as well. Read on and enjoy! (My version of "Go forth and prosper!")

*~Cynthia Richmond*

Author & Editor, *Dream Power: How to Use Your Night Dreams to Change Your Life*, Simon & Schuster

# PREFACE

## DIGGING INTO THE PAST

Have you ever wanted to go on a treasure hunt? If your answer is yes, I invite you to join me here in my new novel. I promise it'll be quite an adventure.

As a person with Spanish and Indian blood (or Mexican, if you prefer), I grew up well versed in my family's history. And although some of the highs in that family history turned into unfair lows, my family always remained very patriotic, with many of us serving in uniform. I was always taught to search for the real history. To look for the real people and stories beyond the simple ones taught in school, and to look for the motivations of the people behind the stories.

Years ago I became a treasure hunter in my spare time, following my childhood dreams. And everywhere I went, I researched the history and read everything I could get my hands on; trying to learn as much as I could. I talked with amateur and expert treasure hunters alike. However, more importantly, I learned a long time ago to enjoy the journey, so that even if I never found my treasure, I would never walk away empty handed. I would be richer for the knowledge and fun gained along the way.

The difficulty in writing this book was in deciding what to include and what to leave out. Much of this story is true or based on real events. However, there were also things that had to be omitted or changed for a variety of reasons; hence the Historical Fiction category. I am obligated to protect others and would never betray that trust bestowed upon me.

One of my greatest concerns in writing this book was the possibility of drawing more people to the locations in the book, since much of this land is sacred to Native Americans. However, in the end, I felt that this was an important story that needed to be told. My hope is that people will always show respect to these sacred places. And that we can all enjoy these lands of our ancestors for many years to come.

I pose a number of questions in this book. Although there are strong male and female characters, they are just like the rest of us and have the same questions. Who do I love? Who am I supposed to be with? What is my purpose in life? What exactly is the 'right thing to do' and why? These are things that drive us all. However, it was James Thurber who perhaps said it best, "It is better to know some of the questions than all of the answers."

My hope is to entertain my readers while taking them on this adventure. And if they learn a thing or two along the way, or find their own questions to ponder, I'll be satisfied.

I hope you enjoy the ride,

*~Lorenzo Rendon*

# Contents

*"Gold is a treasure, and he who possesses it does all he wishes to in this world, and succeeds in helping souls into paradise."*

*—Christopher Columbus*

# Chapter 1

## The Dream

"Keep digging. Keep digging," he heard the voice say, in a deep but loud command. The voice carried eerily over the mountainside. The sound seemed to permeate him, but he did not know the source.

He was inside a dimly lit tunnel. At the end of the tunnel was a wall of rocks that were glowing red-hot. The temperature in the tunnel was sweltering from them. He could see the faces of the men who were walking past him, carrying buckets of water up to the hot rocks. They had long dark hair and dark eyes, but their eyes were lifeless and their faces had blank expressions. He hurried past them to get out of the tunnel. Behind him, he could hear loud popping and cracking of the rocks. Then, as he felt an intense heat on his back, he moved faster out of the tunnel.

Coming out of the tunnel, he looked at his surroundings. It was a large mining operation. There were dozens of people, working all around him. He saw that they were American Indians. The men were moving up and down the mountains in long lines. He could see that they were hauling baskets of rocks and dirt up and down the sides of the mountains. Sweat rolled off their bodies from the hot desert sun as they worked. The desert heat was intense. Most of them were wearing nothing more than loincloths.

But it was their eyes he was drawn to. They were all the same, lifeless, as if they no longer had a soul. It seemed their only existence was to toil for the precious mineral.

"More gold!" the voice boomed again.

Looking around, he saw the source of the voice. A tall figure in a hooded black robe moved closer, towering over his right side. With the sun behind him, the hood of the robe prevented his face from being seen.

Wanting to get away from the hooded figure, he quickly moved into another nearby tunnel. Following the entrance down, he came to an opening. It was well lit, with torches, but this room was filled with people—like the Indians he had seen outside. They stood silently in a circle—they seemed to be staring at something in the center of the room. He moved past them to see what was holding their attention.

It was gold—bars and bars of it, stacked up waist high. It was a mesmerizing sight. It took a moment, but he was able to break his gaze and move back to the tunnel. Looking down the tunnel, he could see the light from the entrance.

"Stay there," the voice said. "I will return. Wait for me."

Just then, he felt a hand on his shoulder. Turning around he could see it was the hand of a young woman.

"What will we do now?" She asked, her face filled with fright.

He heard a loud explosion come from the tunnel's entrance. He could no longer see any light coming from the opening—he knew what that meant. A sense of panic, and helplessness swept over him. Soon they were covered in complete darkness.

"Augh!" Nicholas Rivera yelled aloud as he sat up in bed, in a cold sweat.

His heart was still racing and he was breathing rapidly as he sat there, coming back to consciousness. The room was dark. Quickly he reached for the lamp, and turned on the light. He felt a sense of relief when the light came on.

'What the hell', he thought. 'What kind of dream was that?' He wasn't prone to having dreams so vivid. Or was it a nightmare? Either way, it wasn't normal for him to dream like that. Nick certainly had realistic dreams before, but he hadn't had any for a long time. Not since he came back from the war—and most of those were things he was trying to forget. He always thought it was his subconscious trying to tell him something, but what was *this* dream all about?

Then he remembered the meeting. He looked around his room for the clock—it was on the dresser, next to the bottle of rum. It was almost 7:30 AM. It would take him a couple of hours to drive to Apache Junction. Sleeping late had become a bad habit. Of course, it was easy when you didn't work and you drank till the early morning hours. He got up and went into the bathroom. He started running the water for his shower.

Today was a big day. He was meeting someone for lunch. He hadn't felt like doing much of anything the last few months, but he had been waiting a long time for this meeting.

Maybe this could get his life back on track. After what he had been through, he had to have hope.

A person never knows what the day will bring. However, Nick knew that a person can make a conscious decision every morning to have positive thoughts, and that those thoughts can have the ability to affect the day's events. He just hadn't practiced this in a long time. Today would be a good day to start again. Nick hoped it was going to be a special day, in a good way. But even if it was bad, it might break him out of the rut his life had become. Either way, he sensed that his life was going to change.

After a hot shower, he quickly got dressed. And as he did, he looked around the bedroom. There were family pictures on the wall—pictures of his parents in happier times. His father was more sentimental than he had let on, but he didn't want to think of those things now. He was thinking about his trip. He wanted to make sure he wasn't leaving behind anything he would need.

The small two-bedroom house was his now—the house and the five acres it sat on. He wasn't sure what he was going to do with a house in northern Arizona, but for now he would keep it. He could decide what to do with it later.

He grabbed his black and white Arizona Cardinals cap and put it on. He bought it as a way to feel connected to the state that he was from. Then he grabbed his suitcases and walked out the front door. He wasn't sure when he'd be back—a part of him wanted to start drifting again. At the very least, he would get a room for the night. There was no need to drive down there and back in the same day.

His car was parked around the side of the house—it was a blue Dodge Challenger with a hemi-engine. He found it shortly after coming to Arizona. It was fast and reminded him of the old muscle cars. After loading his suitcases in the trunk, he opened the driver's door and sat down. He put on his sunglasses and started the engine. The hemi-engine rumbled as he gave it some gas. He turned on the radio as he pulled out of the driveway. He found a Classic Rock radio station as he drove along the I-17.

"Here's one from the early eighties," the DJ said. "From the Tarney-Spencer Band called, "No Time to Lose."

Nick turned up the volume. He liked Classic Rock, and this one had a good beat to it.

*We can never understand,*

*We can only be like water:*

*Rolling on to find our way*

*Just get on with the game...*

*It's a game,*

*What a game*

Nick hummed the melody as he drove south down the desert highway. Something about the words resonated with him. He looked at the saguaro cactus, rising up under the clear, blue sky. The sun's rays shot out in between the mountaintops. It was quite a view. It also put him in a good mood, driving down the highway on a beautiful day. It would turn hot later, but for now it was perfect. As he drove along, he repeated the words to the song.

*No time to lose,*
*No time to lose.*

*No time to lose,*
*No time to lose.*

For a guy who had often felt like time was crawling along, he started to get a feeling as if time was going to be a luxury. Why he started to feel that way, he didn't know. Many times he had premonitions or a general sense before major things happened in his life. Was this another?

Apache Junction is a small town just east of Phoenix, Arizona. That's where Sammy McLain asked Nick to meet him. There was a diner located on the edge of town that would not be very busy in the afternoon. They didn't want to attract any attention and they wanted to keep their conversation private.

Nick drove his car into the parking lot. He saw the Florida license plate on the familiar Volvo in front of him and he knew that Sammy was already inside.

It had been an unusually warm fall, but it was now the first part of November and was still warm. He still hadn't got used to the heat and didn't want to leave the comfort of the air-conditioned car. He was wearing a blue, long sleeve Henley™ shirt and blue jeans. He pushed up his shirtsleeves and unbuttoned the collar. Nick had a lot more to deal with than the heat today. He shut off the engine and stepped out of the car. The heat of the sun warmed his face. He walked quickly across the parking lot, to the front door.

Once inside, he found Sammy at a table in the back. He had a briefcase lying on a chair next to him. Sammy was in his mid-forties with greying hair. He was a short man about five foot four with the gift of gab and usually spoke quickly. Today he had on a light colored sport coat and white shoes. His slacks were tan and he wore a bright yellow shirt. Sammy looked like a stereotype of what you might expect someone from Florida to look. The two men shook hands as Nick sat down.

"How are you Nicky?" Sammy asked with a full grin.

"Good."

"Really?"

Nick's brow showed beads of perspiration. "I'm trying to get used to this heat. Christ, it's hot!"

"Wait till the summer. But hey, you're from this part of the country—I thought you'd be used to this. Besides," Sammy added with a chuckle, "it's a dry heat."

Nick rolled his eyes and nodded.

"I haven't lived in this part of the country in years." He said as he wiped the sweat from his brow. "I guess I've been living up north too long." Sammy nodded in agreement.

A waitress approached their table with two glasses of ice water and silverware. She was an attractive young girl with shoulder length blond hair. Sammy gave her a big smile while he ordered his lunch. Nick was too preoccupied to pay her any attention. She tried to make eye contact with him, but he hardly looked at her as he ordered his meal. When she left the table, Sammy was the first one to speak.

"Nicky…Excuse me for saying so, but, you look like hell."

Nick pushed his black hair out of his face. Sammy was right. His hair had grown long and he needed a shave—it wasn't like him. "I've been on vacation," he muttered.

Sammy looked at Nick sympathetically. "I heard about your father... I'm really sorry."

Nick took a sip of his ice water. "Thanks," he said somewhat unemotionally. "But we weren't really all that close."

Sammy wasn't one for prying in to people's emotions. "I understand."

The two men sat there in an awkward silence for a few moments. Then Sammy spoke up.

"Well, let's talk some business, shall we?"

"That's why I'm here," Nick said. "To settle up my money."

"Sure." Sammy said reaching into his sport coat. Smiling he pulled out a check and handed it to Nick.

Nick looked down at the check. His face was expressionless as he studied it. His eyes were glued to the amount—seventy-four thousand dollars. At one time that would have seemed like a lot of money—it still was, but Nick had quite a few debts still to pay. He was especially thinking about paying Jamie her share. Besides, he knew there should be more—a lot more!

Finally, he turned a steely gaze to Sammy and asked, "Is that it?"

"Is that it?" Sammy repeated, surprised. "There's seventy-four thousand dollars there! That's your share. Ask Steve—he's your friend...if you can find him."

"We pulled up ten times that," Nick said slowly, as he looked back at Sammy.

"I told you, there are a lot of expenses on these kinda things."

Nick didn't say anything—he just continued to stare at Sammy with a cool intimidating gaze. It was making Sammy nervous. Nick was about six foot three and weighed about two hundred fifty pounds. He was built solid and his friend, Steve, had told him that he could be very dangerous. He didn't need that kind of problem—this wasn't what he had planned.

Sammy sighed with frustration. "Okay, let me explain all this again." He took a big drink of water and then continued. "First you've got the captain and his crew—that son-of-a-bitch charged us for new pumps and a new motor! That boat was a complete piece-of-shit when we hired him!"

"Hey, that was *your* call," Nick reminded him. "You were the one who said he was a good man."

"I know. I know. Then we had to pay for salvage rights to dive on the wreck site. Plus, we had to pay those college professors just to clean our coins so we could find out how much they're worth. And that's all before you come to the State and Federal Government—you know, everybody's got their hand out looking for a piece of the pie."

Nick grumbled, "You and Steve were supposed to be guarding that pie."

Steven Kelly was an old friend of Nick's who had gotten him involved in the salvage deal. He had moved down to Florida to be closer to the operation.

Nick furrowed his brow with concern. "What you said earlier, about 'if you can find him'—where *is* Steve?"

"Don't know. He dropped out of sight after I gave him his cut. Haven't seen him since."

"That doesn't sound good."

"I don't know..." Then Sammy leaned in towards Nick and said, "Look, nobody is happy about any of this. We all wanted a bigger score, but this isn't bad, and there's a chance that the crew might still bring up more later on—they're still finding a coin here and there. You just have to be patient."

Nick was now feeling exasperated. "I've waited a year and a half! I have people to pay back now," he said, leaning back in his chair.

Sammy held his hand up to halt the conversation. "I understand," he said, conceding the point. "But, you have to remember... there are other deals out there." He said in a singsong tone.

"Other deals?" Nick asked. "Like what?"

A smile came over Sammy's face as he reached into his briefcase and pulled out a manila folder. He pushed it across the table to Nick. "Like this."

Nick looked down at the folder but didn't open it up. "What is it?" he said somewhat curious.

"It's a new deal!" Sammy said enthusiastically, with a slight grin.

Nick folded his arms in skepticism and prompted, "Go on..."

"A mountain—a mountain full of gold!" Sammy said with hushed excitement, as he looked for Nick's facial expression.

Nick was still skeptical. "A mountain full of gold?" He snickered, incredulous. "What, you mean like the 'Lost Dutchman's Gold'?"

"Shhh!" Sammy looked over both his shoulders and then nodded. "It's a good possibility. It's all in there, all the research." he said pointing to the folder. "Read it and decide for yourself."

"And how do I fit into this?" Nick pointed to the file.

"Okay, let me explain it. I've been working on this for several years—I really did my homework on this one. We had the best research, men, and equipment—I knew we were going to hit a home run—we were really getting close."

"So, what happened?"

"Well," Sammy said, leaning forward, trying to choose his words carefully, "they got scared." He hushed.

"Scared?"

"Yeah, scared off."

Not sure of what he was hearing, Nick asked, "Scared of what?"

"Ghosts maybe? Who knows—Indian curses? It's in the Superstition Mountains for Chrissake! Everybody around here believes in that shit! That's why I wanted to meet you here—I know you can find it. If anyone can pull this off, you can. A guy like you, you aren't going to get scared. You're familiar with the desert." Sammy continued as he sat back in his chair, smiling. "You're the perfect guy for something like this… and you'll be famous."

Nick shook his head and slid the folder back toward Sammy. "I don't want to be famous. I have other plans."

"Like what?" Sammy taunted. "Drifting around aimlessly? Doesn't sound like much of a plan if you ask me."

Sammy's words were cutting, but Nick knew he was right. Drifting around wasn't much of a plan. Fact was, he had no real plans of what to do, even after he paid the loans back.

"Just read it." Sammy pleaded. "But, it has to be done this summer; the military's trying to annex the land for a artillery range."

"This summer?" Nick said, incredulous.

"Yes, by August 1st."

"Let me get this straight," Nick said with skepticism. "I'm just suppose to go wandering around the middle of the desert in the hottest time of the year, and find a lost treasure that nobody's been able to find for over a hundred years. A treasure that may, or may not, be nothing more than a legend. And, overcome any Indian curses that may have been placed upon it. And get it all done in the next few months?"

"Well, when you say it like that—"

Nick cut him off, "You're crazy!"

"Just look at it!" Sammy pleaded.

"Sammy, even if I was foolish enough to do something like that, I can't afford to get into another deal."

"No, no. This won't cost you anything out of pocket, just your time."

This sounded too good to be true, and knowing Sammy, it probably was. "No one else involved, just you and me?" Nick asked.

"The previous investors have all walked away."

"So, now you come to me?" Nick said, still suspicious.

Sammy nodded his head in agreement, but didn't say anything. He didn't want to appear desperate.

"It'll still take a crew, equipment, expenses. You gonna pay for all that?"

"Within reason—a small crew, not some goddamned army. Now… you want in?"

Nick pulled the file closer and opened it, scanning what looked like pages of charts and maps. "What about the split?" He asked.

"You get one third." Sammy said, thinking it sounded like a reasonable split—he didn't want to drive too hard of a bargain. Then he quickly added, "Your crew gets paid out of your share."

"One third?" Nick chuckled. "You *must* be desperate."

Sammy chose to ignore Nick's suspicion. "Do we have a deal?"

Nick flipped through some of the papers in the file. "If I do it—I want half."

"Half?" Sammy objected.

"Expenses out of your half and I'll pay the crew shares out of mine."

Sammy paused—calculating figures in his head—then rolled his eyes and asked again, "So, are you in?"

Nick slapped the file closed. "I'll think about it."

"Sure. Sure. Take a couple of days. Read through the material. Let me know if you want to go out there."

"Where can I contact you?" Nick asked.

"I'm staying at our Base camp—an old construction site we use, not far from here. The address and number is in the file." Sammy continued. "Now, think about it… but I'm telling you—you can't afford to pass this up!"

Nick looked at the folder then back at Sammy with some doubt. "Hmmm." He knew Sammy was the consummate salesman. "Yeah, where've I heard *that* before?"

As Nick stood up and walked out of the café, he suddenly remembered the strange dream he had last night. 'What did it mean?' He wondered to himself. 'Could it be related to this deal?'

# Chapter 2
## The Superstitions

Nick had found a cheap motel to stay in for a while. After waking, he stepped into the bathroom, standing in front of the sink and mirror. It was 6:30 AM. He hadn't been up this early in a long time. He washed his face and then stood there, staring at his own reflection. He hadn't really looked at himself in awhile, and it was just as well. He didn't like what he was seeing; his hair was too long and he needed a shave. The months of hard drinking had made his face look puffy. His body wasn't as hard as it should be—he hadn't trained in the Dojo in a long time. It was time to make some changes.

He dug out his sweats and a sleeveless t-shirt from his suitcase and put them on. He started with push-ups, doing as many as he could on his knuckles. Then he did sit-ups until his stomach muscles burned like fire. After some stretches, it was out the door and over to the road for a long run. During the run, he knew he could organize his thoughts. So much had happened in the past year. So, he tried to focus and put things into perspective. He ran down a long dirt road, quickly loosing himself in his thoughts.

At thirty-four, his life wasn't exactly where he thought it should be. As hard as it was to admit, he probably hadn't handled things very well recently. Maybe he had been denying his depression. Was that why he numbed his mind with alcohol?

His father had been sick for months before he ultimately passed. The doctors said it was complications of the heart and liver. However, Nick knew it was all the years of drinking and hard living.

They never had a close relationship; and after Nick joined the Marines, he didn't come home to Arizona very much. He had grown up not far from where he was, but he had never really cared for the desert. So, when he got the chance, he left. He moved far to the north, to Alaska. Maybe it was just as well—his father was a difficult man to be around.

His mother certainly thought so—she divorced him years before. Nick's mother had died from breast cancer a few years earlier. And even though his father had passed more recently, it was his mother that he missed the most. She always seemed to have the right words of encouragement for him.

And there was Jamie, his ex-girlfriend. At least he would have the money to pay her back now—or at least pay most of it back.

As he began pacing himself in his long run, getting into a rhythm, he pondered about his future.

*If I were able to somehow find this treasure, money wouldn't be an issue anymore. Now, what would that be like; to be rich and never have to worry about money again; to come and go as I pleased; never have to take orders from anyone again? I can only imagine a life like that.*

*I could help my friend with his Dojo; advertise in the papers; maybe fly the students to some of the bigger tournaments. Master Kisae is a good man. He deserves something like that.*

*And I wouldn't have to go back to my job at the Prison—with all of those office pukes second-guessing the guys on the front lines. That's what started my spiral to begin with. But I couldn't do anything about that. And I don't want to start thinking about it again, not now.*

He thought about all of those things as he ran along the desert road. He tried to put it all into perspective. Understand it, and then move on. His training had taught him that life wasn't going to wait. It was going to come at him with new challenges, whether he was ready or not. That was the thought that stuck in his head as he sprinted back to his motel room, finishing his run.

After a hot shower, he brushed his teeth and shaved—the haircut would have to wait. While getting dressed, he noticed the bottle of rum on the nightstand. Drinking himself to sleep had become a habit. But, he hadn't had a drink in days, since the meeting with Sammy. He didn't want to be tempted, so he grabbed the bottle and poured the sweet liquor down the sink. He needed to think with a clear head now.

His motel room had a table and two chairs next to the bed. The contents of the folder were scattered across the table and bed. Nick had been studying for two days. There were photos of a mountain and the surrounding area. Some were pictures of treasure maps that no one had been able to decipher. There were reports from researchers, notes from workers, excerpts from books, stories about lost treasures and gold. Everyone had an opinion as to what the key was to finding the gold.

Nick reflected on how every one of them believed the gold was there. However, this was natural for men who are hunting for gold. "Gold fever" was the term many used to describe what men like that were going through. Gold could become an obsession—and one that Nick was starting to understand.

He began reading some of the stories. The most famous one was *The Legend of the Lost Dutchman Mine*.

According to the story, Jacob Waltz and his partners found a rich goldmine. On one occasion, Waltz left his partners to go to town for supplies. He claimed that when he returned to his camp, the Apaches had killed all his partners. Many doubted his story and believed instead that Waltz himself had killed them. What was certain, however, was that Waltz would leave Phoenix for his mine and then return several days later with high-grade ore.

Years later when he got sick, on his deathbed he gave confusing directions to his mine. Yet, many people who have studied the maps and evidence believed it to be in the Weaver's Needle area.

Nick continued reading through the file folder. There were stories about a Spanish ruling family, the Peraltas. They supposedly had a number of gold mines in the area before they were all massacred in 1847.

Then there were the stories of the Jesuit priests, who were also alleged to have gold mines. However, those stories were fuzzier. For two reasons; one, they were much older stories, and two, the Jesuits were very secretive—so much of the information on them is pieced together from historical documents and expert speculation.

There were even some writings on things that happened to the last crew. Vehicles and equipment would stop running for no apparent reason. Some of the men reported having horrible nightmares. One man even reported seeing a head floating in the preview screen of his video camera. If the stories were true, it was no wonder they got scared off. Nick found all of it fascinating, but there were two things that really caught his attention.

One was a geological report by a man named George Rogers. Sammy had hired Rogers after some other treasure hunters had recommended him. He had made some interesting claims in his report. It appeared that he had used some expensive infrared and thermal imagery equipment as well as sophisticated modeling software to reach his conclusions.

The other thing that caught his attention was a group of photos taken of petroglyphs in the area. Unfortunately, the pictures were of poor quality. So, he wanted to take a closer look at them.

Nick sat down on one of the chairs and started looking through the notes. He wanted more information. He found the phone number for Sammy, and called him.

Sammy answered his phone in a chipper tone. “Hello?”

“Hey, it’s me.”

“Well, what do you think?” Sammy asked, impatiently.

“Well, you’ve got my curiosity.”

“Yeah?”

“Yeah,” Nick confirmed. “But I want to go in and take a look at something first.”

“What’s that?”

Nick picked up one of the photos and squinted at it. “Right before your workers left, they found some petroglyphs not far from the mountain—”

Sammy cut Nick off, “Right, they found some drawings on a rock, off to the right of the other ones. They were thinking that maybe those petroglyphs might hold the key.”

Nick picked up the stack of pictures and thumbed through them. “It’s possible.” He said in a very focused tone.

Sammy’s curiosity was piqued, “Possible?” He asked excitedly.

“I’d feel better if I checked it out.”

"Tell you what..." Sammy began. "Come out here to the camp. There's a jeep you can use if you want to go out there. You'll need a four-wheel drive to get through the rocky terrain."

The Superstition Mountains sit to the east of Phoenix. The Mountains are rugged and rocky. Although they are full of Saguaro cactus and brush, they offer little else in the way of plant life. The lack of water and extreme heat makes it difficult for much of anything else to grow. The Indians believed the Mountains were Sacred.

In 1540 the Spaniard Francisco Vázquez de Coronado, explored this area. He was looking for the legendary Seven Golden Cities of Cibola. While legend has it that Coronado explored the mountains, it has never been documented. More likely, he sent his Lieutenant and some men in to explore the mountains while the main body of his expedition went east. According to the legend, some of his men were driven mad. Others disappeared. The Spaniards were soon convinced that the mountains were cursed. And since no gold was found, they left, and traveled north. But, the Mountains would be henceforth known as the Superstition Mountains.

Nick signed the Government logbook at the start of the gravel road leading up into the Mountains. This was to help track someone if they got lost. And occasionally the military did some live fires in the area. They didn't want any civilians around when they did that.

He had been driving up the mountain road for hours. It wasn't much more than a Jeep trail really. In places it was steep and rocky, so the drive had been pretty slow. The Jeep had half doors, and no top, so at times it was very dusty. He didn't know in actual miles how far he had driven. He did have a topographical map that he used. Occasionally he stopped to orient himself. There were numerous trails that crisscrossed each other. And since he wasn't familiar with the area, he wanted to make sure he was on the right trail.

It was mid-day before he found the right location; a place called Deadhorse canyon; a wide canyon with a foot trail leading up to the Western Wall. He double-checked the coordinates with his map and compass. Satisfied, he parked the Jeep as far off the trail as he could. He would have to walk the rest of the way. It was a warm day but he was dressed for it. He wore a cotton vest over a T-shirt with Cargo pants. Nick grabbed his camera and stuffed it in his vest before he headed up the trail.

The trail led him up a steep incline, perhaps a quarter of a mile. Straight to the canyon's rock wall before turning and running parallel with it. He walked several yards along the wall before he saw the first petroglyph. He saw white markings on a rock that looked like an animal with horns. He pulled out his camera and began to take photographs. As he walked along, he began to see more and more. Some were faded and hard to see. Many were symbols he was unfamiliar with. He took special care to photograph them at the best angle for viewing, the more contrast, the better. The petroglyphs covered an area about ten yards long. Nick photographed them all, continuing until his 35-mm camera was out of film.

He headed back down the trail to the jeep. He was halfway down the hill when he noticed them. Two vehicles had pulled up behind the Jeep, with a couple of men walking around it. Nick suspected possible trouble with these guys. He stopped in his tracks, wondering what they wanted. He thought about his options. Quickly, he realized that he didn't have any. Nick was going to have to confront them. If there was going to be trouble, maybe they would be overconfident. Hopefully, they were just curious, he thought as he walked down the hill.

"Hello," Nick said, walking up to the men.

"Good afternoon," one of the men said, lighting a cigarette. Standing next to the Jeep, he appeared to be in charge. "Is this your vehicle?"

"Yes, it is. But I'm leaving now so…sorry if I blocked your way."

There was one man to Nick's left. The man in charge was in front of him, and a large man was to his right. Back farther behind the large man were two more men who had come out from one of the trucks.

"Oh no. We just thought maybe your vehicle had broken down. Or maybe you were lost. The desert can be an unforgiving place," He continued, inhaling off his dark cigarette.

"Well, I appreciate the concern," Nick said with a forced smile, "but the vehicle's fine and I'm not lost."

"Wonderful," the leader said. "But tell me, Señor, what are you doing out here?"

"Taking pictures of plant life," Nick said. He pulled the camera out of his vest pocket, and then shoved it back down. "I'm a Botanist."

"Excellent. Allow me to introduce myself. My name is Diego Alameda; I own a granite mine not far from here. These men work for me. And who might you be?"

"My name?" Nick asked. "Montana... Joe Montana. And unless I'm mistaken, this is all government land."

"Yes, Mr. Montana you are right. Now, we don't get many Botanists out here. You see, this can be a very dangerous land. In fact, I would recommend you not come out here again.

"Oh Yeah?" Nick said. "Thanks for the tip. Well, gotta go."

"Of course," Diego said. "Just hand over the camera and you can be on your way."

"The camera?" Nick asked.

"Hand it to me." Diego said extending his hand out. When Nick didn't move, he signaled to the big man.

The large man reached out with his left hand to grab Nick. When he did, Nick deflected his arm and landed a punch on his ribs. He then delivered a kick to the side of the man's left knee, causing it to buckle. Nick then grabbed his shoulders. The big man was completely off balance. The two men that had been leaning on the truck were now running right at them. When they got close Nick pushed the big man into them. Remembering that there was another man behind him, he spun around quickly. Just in time to face the man who was running right at him. Nick took a step to the side and guided the man into his three companions. Bodies were bouncing into each other and falling backwards.

It was all over fairly quickly, Nick thought. He looked down at the four men struggling to get up. It was then that he heard the pistol being cocked in his left ear.

"Enough!" Diego said. "The camera, cabrón."

Nick reached into his vest and pulled out the camera. He needed a distraction.

"Here," Nick said, flipping the camera in the air towards Diego. Diego's attention turned to catching the camera. That was all that Nick needed. In a split second he grabbed the gun and twisted it out of Diego's hand, and caught the camera as it was falling. Now he held the gun to Diego's head.

Nick backed all the men away and then fired the gun at their lead vehicle, putting a hole in the radiator. He quickly jumped in his jeep and sped off.

"Damn", he thought, as he heard their guns go off, "I should have checked them for weapons." He looked in the mirror to see one man shooting at him while the others were pushing the vehicle he damaged out of the way. "Who are these guys?" He wondered. "And why would they want to kill me for just looking around?"

He wasn't able to go fast on the mountain trail; there were so many turn-offs, he couldn't be sure he wasn't lost. And to make things worse, the men he was running from had easily pushed the first vehicle out of the way and were speeding after him in the second car. They were gaining ground on him. He was going to have to do something if he was to elude them.

"Faster, faster!" Diego yelled at his driver. "I want that bastard!"

Diego watched as they got closer and closer to the jeep. When they were about two hundred yards behind it, one of his men started shooting from out of the window.

The trail turned to the left when Nick saw him. An old Indian man suddenly appeared out of nowhere. He was a ghostly figure with long white hair and a purple headband. He was standing on the trail with his hands up, like he was blocking the path. Nick had to do something and quickly, to avoid running him over.

Diego and his men were still gaining ground. They had closed the distance to about one hundred yards. But now they watched, as the jeep made a sharp right turn up the mountainside. His driver slowed down as the jeep seemed to fly off the mountain.

"What the hell?" Diego said as their vehicle came to a halt.

"I must have hit him Boss," said Thomas, the one who fired out the window.

"Yes, I think so," Diego agreed, unable to think of any other reason the jeep would turn so erratically.

"Go check it out." He told the men.

Thomas and the driver walked to the top of the hill. Smoke was already rising from the jeep. It lay overturned in the bottom of a deep ravine. No one could survive a crash like that, they thought. They came back down the hill joking and laughing. His fighting tricks couldn't save him from a crash like that. Thomas was all too happy to tell his boss what they had seen.

"Well," Diego said, thinking hard. He would have liked to search for the camera. But one of his men had a dislocated arm, and another, a damaged knee. "I don't suppose there is any more we can do here. ¡Vámonos!" He said to the driver.

Soon the vehicle was heading back in the direction it had come from.

# Chapter 3

## The Girl, the Priest, and the DEA

Cheyenne Woods loved spending time outdoors in the Desert Mountains. After a hectic week of work, it was nice to spend her Saturday afternoon out rock climbing. Out in the desert, with no one else around, she could escape the problems of the world for a while.

She had only been climbing for about a year, but with her strong toned body, she excelled at it. She liked to challenge herself physically. She had found this canyon a few weeks before, and it had some rock faces that she thought would be perfect to try out.

Cheyenne checked the carabiner on her safety line before climbing up a few feet higher. When she found a secure spot, she stopped to take a break. She closed her eyes, enjoying the peace and quiet. She could only hear the wind whistling through the canyon…and the faint roar… of an engine! It was getting louder and louder, like it was coming right at her! But how could that be possible? She opened her eyes in time to see the vehicle flying in the air, down the canyon overhead.

"Oh my God," she thought as she clung tightly to the rocks. She watched the vehicle sail over her and crash down into the canyon below. She clung to the rocks, almost frozen for a minute, as she realized what must have happened. "I better get down there," she thought. "Someone could be hurt."

When Nick jumped from the vehicle as it flew through the air, he tried to roll as far away out of sight, as he could. It was his only hope of getting away. He hit the rocks hard. And now he lay there, on a jagged ledge, in pain from his head and chest. How long he lay there, he couldn't be sure. He was still groggy when he opened his eyes. He was surprised to see the face of a pretty girl staring down on him with concerned green eyes.

Nick lifted his head up to get a better look at the girl, and the surroundings. She had long, dark hair, and was wearing a brown cotton shirt and khaki shorts. He was eye level with her brown hiking boots, and there was a hiking stick lying next to her backpack. She was obviously well prepared. That was good.

"Where am I?" He asked, not sure of his surroundings.

The girl, who had been kneeling over him, raised her head. She looked around the spacious mountain range.

"I call this place heaven." She answered with a smile and then looked back down at him.

"Heaven? Well, then, you must be an angel." Nick said, only half joking. His head was clearing, but he could still feel a sharp pain in his chest.

"No." She smirked. "I'm still working on my wings. How about you?" She asked.

"I'm no angel," Nick admitted, clinching his side. "But if you call this place heaven, you gotta be crazy."

"You drive your jeep off a cliff, and you call me crazy?" She countered playfully.

"What about the old man?" Nick asked concerned, suddenly remembering the old Indian. "Is he okay?"

"I didn't see any old man," she said, looking at him puzzled.

Nick was confused. Just what the hell had he seen? He wondered.

"What are you doing out here anyway?" She asked, noticing the camera Nick had slung around his neck.

She picked it up and held it in her hand. When she did, he quickly grabbed her arm. Startling her, she quickly dropped it.

Nick let go of her arm and composed himself. "Just out taking pictures." He said. "What about you?"

"Rock climbing. It's a funny thing," she said looking around, "it's not the prettiest place in Arizona, but I always seem to get drawn out here. I can't really explain it."

"Speaking of Heaven or Hell, I might see one of them sooner than I want, unless we get out of here." Nick was thinking more of the men who were chasing him, than of his injuries.

"How did you happen to find me?" He asked.

"Well, I was climbing on the side of that rock face and saw your Jeep go flying down over me. I went back to check out the wreckage, but I didn't find anyone. So, I figured I better start looking around. Lucky I found you." She said, looking back at Nick.

She gave him some water from the canteen she carried. Nick drank up, before she asked if he could walk.

"I think so." He said, struggling to get up. "My chest is killing me."

"You might have some cracked ribs," she said as she helped him up. "I have a truck not far from here."

"Okay."

"Here, take this," she said as she handed him her hiking stick. Slowly, they began working their way off the ledge and down the canyon.

At Superior Medical Center, in a town with the same name, Nick received the news. He had two fractured ribs and a mild concussion. After wrapping his ribs, the doctor said they wanted him to stay the night for observation. The girl had been waiting for word about him. She came into the room when she found out he was staying overnight.

"I have to go," she said, putting a piece of paper down on the desk, next to his bed. "And you need some rest, Nick is it?"

"Yes, Nick Rivera. Wait," he said. "What's your name?"

"My real name's Lynn, but everyone calls me Cheyenne."

She said with a smile, and pointed to the card. "You ever want to go for a hike again, let me know."

She smiled looking down at him again, before walking away. But it was an unusual smile. Like she knew something he didn't.

Nick slept soundly through the night, and woke refreshed considering the circumstances. His ribs still hurt, but everything else was fine. After getting an okay" from the nurse, he got dressed, gathered his things and went to the discharge desk down the hall.

He was signing papers for his personal things when two men approached him.

"Mr. Rivera?" The one closest to Nick said.

"Yes?" Nick replied, turning to look at them.

The nearest one was a short, young Hispanic. The other was a large white kid, with blonde hair. He was taller than Nick, and seemed to have an arrogant smile on his face. They were both in their twenties, with short hair. With their dark suits, Nick figured them for government agents. They didn't need to, but they both showed him their badges—they were DEA agents.

"I'm agent Diaz, and this is agent Hanson," the smaller one said, nodding towards his partner. "We'd like to talk with you."

"What do you want to talk to me about?" Nick asked.

"Actually, it's our boss. He'd like to speak with you. He's waiting at our office. Please, we'll have more privacy there."

"Okay, but I don't have a car here."

"That's fine." Diaz continued, "We have a car right outside."

Before they left, agent Diaz turned to the girl behind the desk.

"Thanks Donna," he said.

The three men walked out and got into the dark-green government sedan and drove to Phoenix. Nick sat in the back seat, staring out the window. He thought about the two agents sitting in the front seat. Agent Hanson was driving. If they were going to ask him about drugs, they were wasting their time. More likely, they were interested in the same men he had run into in the mountains. Better to talk with them, and find out who he was dealing with. Besides, he needed a ride back to town anyway.

Other than the agents arguing about the music on the radio, they rode mostly in silence. When they did talk with him, again, it was Diaz.

"We're taking you to our downtown office. Special Agent Goldberg wants to speak with you."

"About what?" Nick asked, not really expecting an answer. These two were obviously low-level errand boys. They seemed too young to be heading up a major DEA investigation.

"I'll let Goldberg explain things. " Then without skipping a beat, Diaz changed the subject. "He said you were an Alaska State Trooper. Is that right?"

"I was." Nick replied.

“I heard those guys were bad ass.” agent Hanson said, speaking to Nick directly for the first time. Hanson looked at him in the rear view mirror, watching for a response, but Nick kept staring out the window.

Nick was wondering why the DEA would want to talk with him? He didn’t have any special ability or knowledge that could help them. However, maybe he could learn something useful from them. He knew that when cops talked with you, it was usually a one way flow of information. They normally didn’t tell you anymore than they had to. He would have to find an opportunity to ask them some questions.

As he looked out the window at nothing in particular, a smile slowly came to Nick’s face. He was thinking how his life had taken an interesting turn this week. He wasn’t sure if it was good or bad. But at least it was different. After months of being ambivalent about everything, he was starting to feel a spark of excitement again.

They rode the final minutes in silence, until they came to the large federal building. Agent Hanson entered his code at the gate and drove into the underground garage. After parking, they took the elevator to the first floor. This gave Nick the idea that their operation was temporary—they wouldn’t be around long enough to even get an office with a view from the upper floors.

After walking halfway down the hall, they walked in to an outer office. There they checked in with Goldberg’s receptionist. She picked up her phone and told him they had arrived, before allowing them through the second door. The agents motioned Nick to go ahead of them.

Nick looked around as he entered the office. The office was large, but not well lit. As if windows had been an afterthought. The walls were sparsely covered, and files seemed to cover what few tables there were. Knowing government pecking orders, Nick knew that it meant that Goldberg was either only here temporarily or that he was a low-level employee. Nick hoped it was the latter.

Next, Nick saw that there were two men waiting in the office. The one sitting behind the desk he presumed was Goldberg. He was sitting in a large leather chair, but the desk was a plain-black government issue. He was a short, heavy set, balding man, with glasses. He didn't look like a DEA agent.

The other man sat in a leather chair to the side of Goldberg's desk. He was an older man with thinning grey hair and wire rimmed glasses. He appeared to be tall and thin. He wore a light colored shirt, and khaki pants. Since he was not wearing a suit, Nick wondered if he was with the government as well. Nick didn't think he was, but he was going to find out.

The man behind the desk kept his head down, as he looked over a file in front of him. It took him a few moments before he looked up and acknowledged them.

"Yes, yes, come in." Goldberg said. "You must be Mr. Rivera."

"I am. "Nick replied, walking towards the desk.

"I'm Special Agent Goldberg." He said, rising to shake Nick's hand. "And this is Father Jericho Martin." He said, motioning to the man on his right. "Please, have a seat."

He said, motioning to one of the two large chairs in front of the desk.

Nick sat down, but the other two agents remained standing behind him. He looked at the agent's desk. On one side, next to a desk lamp was a picture of his family. On the other side was something unusual. It was a paperweight with the saying "Figures don't lie and Liars don't figure" on it. Nick thought it was an odd mantra for a DEA agent.

"I've been reviewing your file." Goldberg continued. "Very interesting."

Nick was surprised and raised his right eyebrow. "My file?"

"Yes, I like to know who I'm dealing with, you know." Goldberg continued. "It's all in here."

"It is?" Nick asked, curious as to what they thought they knew.

"Oh yes," Goldberg began reading the information. "Nickolas Rivera, age thirty-four, graduated from Chandler High School here in Phoenix, where you were a star athlete. You then enlisted in the Marine Corps and served four years—two tours of combat, one in Iraqi, one in Afghanistan—winner of the Bronze Star. When you got out, you moved to Alaska, where you attended college. You worked for a number of private security jobs before becoming an Alaska State Trooper. But then you left the troopers to work in the prisons. You became a Sargent with the Department of Corrections, where you served until nine months ago. You resigned after charges of excessive use of force. Now you run a karate school in Anchorage."

Nick quickly added defensively, "I was cleared of all charges."

"Uh huh." Goldberg said, uninterested. "Does that about sum it up?"

A slight smug look grew on Nick's face, "Well, not everything."

"Oh?" Goldberg cocked his head. "Please fill us in."

"Well, my most important work..." Nick paused and started faking a serious tone as they all looked on in anticipation. "I had a paper route when I was ten. Now that was a critical job. Getting up that early, hitting all the right houses..."

Nick thought he saw a slight smirk on Goldberg's face. But the other agents found no humor in it.

"Smart ass!" Hanson growled, as he hit Nick hard with an open hand on the back of his head.

Nick turned quickly to stand up and confront him. However, as he turned, he felt a sharp stabbing pain in his chest from his injured ribs. Nick grimaced and remained seated. Sitting still, he had almost forgotten about his injuries. As much as he wanted to, this wasn't the time to be fighting.

"Augh," Nick moaned, more from the pain in his chest than the blow from Hanson.

"Hanson!" Goldberg yelled. "Stop it!"

Hanson backed up reluctantly. He didn't like this guy being disrespectful. This was serious business. He wanted to make sure that Nick knew that they meant business.

"Sarcasm. I can appreciate that." Goldberg said. "But I can assure you this is a very serious issue.

Nick started getting frustrated, "Look, what the hell do you want anyway?"

"I want to help you."

"Help me?" Nick said skeptically.

Goldberg continued, "Yes, you help me and I'll help you."

Nick squinted in confusion. "With what?"

"Information." Goldberg said, as a smile came to his face. "Look, you go digging around out there without the right permits and paperwork, the government could shut you down—confiscate anything you might find."

Nick started looking for a way to exit the topic, "Look, I appreciate your offer but—"

Goldberg quickly cut him off and snaps, "Hey, we know you aren't here to get a suntan! I think you're here looking for treasure in the Superstitions."

Nick sat back in his chair expressionless, saying nothing; just listening.

"I got a call not long ago from a friend in the FBI's office. Seems some hikers found a body out there, with the head decapitated. I figure it was done by the same people you had a run-in with."

Goldberg slid a picture in front of him. It was a photo of Diego, the leader of the men who had chased him.

"Do you recognize this man?" Goldberg asked knowingly.

Nick looked Goldberg in the eye without emotion. "No."

Goldberg continued, "That is Diego Alameda; made his money smuggling drugs in from Mexico. He bought a rock quarry out there. But, mostly he spends his time looking for treasure in the Superstitions. Coincidentally, he showed up about a year ago, about the same time the FBI started finding bodies out there."

"That's all very interesting, but what does it have to do with me?" Nick grumbled.

"You weren't out there hunting for treasure?" Goldberg asked suspiciously.

Again, Nick just looked at him coldly saying, "No."

Goldberg opened a file from his desk and flipped through some pages. "Tell me, do you know a 'Sammy McLain'?" he asked, looking over his glasses at Nick without lifting his head.

Nick didn't answer, but Goldberg had this part planned. He pulled out a newspaper clipping from the file. It was from the Daytona Tribune. It was a picture of Nick with Sammy, Steve, and their boat Captain, Manny Maluu. They were holding up handfuls of the gold coins their crew found.

Then looking Nick up and down, Goldberg nodded at him, "Your injuries; a crashed vehicle, registered to McLain—hikers reported it."

Nick looked away. Then flippantly tossed back at him, "Just out four-wheeling." He forced a smile. Then leaning forward in his chair, with a determined look on his face, he asks, "But now, I have a question for you. Why is the DEA interested in treasure?"

"Oh, Mr. Rivera," Goldberg chuckled, "I'm not with the Drug Enforcement Agency. I'm with the Internal Revenue Service."

"The IRS?" Nick said bewildered, trying to piece it together.

"Now, my associates here, they are with the DEA," Goldberg said motioning to the two agents still standing behind Nick. "I'm a C.I., a Criminal Investigator with the IRS. This is a joint operation."

Nick then concluded, "So, basically you're here to see that the government gets its share of anything that's found. No matter who finds it? Is that right?"

"That's right. Now, you're an ex-cop—one of the good guys, like us. But you have a questionable partner." Goldberg said, half-smiling.

"Well, we all have our burdens, don't we," Nick said almost under his breath and turning his head to look at Hanson for a moment.

"And what about you?" Nick asked, now looking at the older man, who just sat there listening intently. "What's your interest in all of this?"

"I'm an archeologist for the Catholic Church." Father Martin replied. "You see if there were to be any human remains found, the Church would be very interested,"

"By Catholic Church, I'm guessing you're a Jesuit?" Nick said.

Father Martin nodded his head, "I was in the Jesuit Order—I am mostly retired now. I do consulting work like this sometimes for the government."

"Consulting?" Nick seemed puzzled. He wanted to find out just who this guy really was.

"You see," Father Martin continued. "If there were any human remains found. Well, you would have to be shut down and professionals would have to take over the site."

"Interesting…" Nick chose his next words carefully; these guys weren't the only ones who knew how to interrogate someone. "But what makes you think that there would be any bodies found?"

"Well," Father Martin said, looking uncomfortable now. "One never knows what might turn up at one of these old sites."

Nick saw the discomfort in his face as he spoke, but he wanted to keep pressing him. He needed all the information he could get. And Father Martin seemed like a man who had a lot of information.

"Sure, but why would the church be concerned about bodies being buried in an old gold mine? I mean, unless they think maybe it had something to do with the Jesuits. There are lots of legends about them."

Everyone was looking at Father Martin now, but he seemed to be flustered by the question. He needed to be cautious in his response. To these people he was merely an advisor.

"I am an archeologist. I have worked on many dig sites around the world. The Church has always taken an interest in history. And yes, there are many legends of Jesuit mines—fabrications mostly. My interest is in bringing the true history to light." Father Martin explained.

Nick prodded, "The *true* history?"

"Yes, I'm afraid that the reality of our history usually proves less colorful than the legends we often hear about. Most often legends originate from those with active imaginations."

"So, you're interested in history, and you're interested in a drug dealer?" Nick said, now looking back to agent Goldberg.

"Actually, these two fine DEA agents are interested in the drug dealer." Goldberg said, motioning to the two agents behind Nick. "As I said, this is a joint task force, but I'm the one that's interested in the gold."

"Oh, that's right," Nick said sarcastically. "Gold that you wouldn't get a cut of, unless someone else took all the risk to find it."

"The government's going to get their share, I'll make sure of it. That's my job," Goldberg said confidently.

"That's nice," Nick feigned disinterest. "But I'm not hunting treasure. And as far as this Alameda guy—haven't seen him."

"You're sure?" Goldberg asked with suspicion.

"Yeah," Nick tried to sound convincing, nodding his head. "Can I go now?"

Goldberg frowned and crooked his mouth then quickly relaxed his face. “Sure,” he said coolly, as he slid his business card across his desk. “Tell you what, if you hear of anything, give me a call.”

Nick picked up the card. “Sure,” he said glancing at it. He then shot up out of the chair and walked to the door.

As Nick was on his way out of the office, agent Diaz followed him into the hallway.

“Hey man,” Diaz said. “I’m sorry, but my partner doesn’t like you.”

“Yeah? Could have fooled me.” Nick said sardonically.

“I’m not like him.” Diaz insisted.

“Yeah? What do you care what I think?”

“I don’t know,” Diaz shrugged. “Maybe I think you were a good cop.”

“That depends on who you talk to,” Nick mumbled. “Look, I don’t know you, but you’re probably a good agent. So you’ve got a crappy partner. You’re not the first guy that’s happened to.”

“Yeah.” Diaz nodded.

“Maybe you’ll catch a break on this case and get reassigned.” Nick said reassuringly.

“I don’t know.” Diaz said with a dejected tone.

“Look, maybe we can help each other.” Nick said. “Tell you what, if I hear anything, I’ll let you know.”

“Okay. Hey, can I give you a ride somewhere?” The young agent asked, feeling better now.

“Sure.”

Agent Diaz drove him back to his motel. After he dropped him off, Nick called Sammy.

“Where have you been?” Sammy asked concerned.

“I was meeting with some of your friends!” Nick said mockingly.

“My friends?” Sammy feigned ignorance. “Who?”

“Your friends with the Feds. And I also met the ones with the guns and the Spanish accents.”

“Yeah? Uh, are you still in?” Sammy asked sheepishly.

Nick paused then grumbled, “Yeah, I’m in. But my price has just gone up! And, oh yeah, there was a little problem with your Jeep...”

# Chapter 4

## The Vision Quest

Nick had to find her. She had probably saved his life, getting him down off that mountain. He wanted to find her and thank her in person. In his mind, a simple phone call just wouldn't cut it. He found directions to the name of the bar on the business card she gave him. He thought to himself, she probably waited tables, or maybe bartended there.

As he drove down the gravel road, he came upon a bar named "Rockers". It was a big building, with dark wooden siding. The gravel parking lot was full, but then, it was a Saturday night. He hoped she was there working.

Walking inside, he found the bar was packed. The clientele wasn't upscale, but it did seem to be a mixture of people from different backgrounds. Nick had certainly been in rougher places. There was a long L-shaped bar on one side with several bartenders behind it. On the other side was a stage and large dance floor, with tables scattered all around. There was a band onstage playing loud Rock songs. But Nick was intent on making his way to the bar. After a few minutes, he finally got the attention of one of the bartenders.

She was an attractive brunette in a leather skirt and halter-top. The tattoos on her arms gave her an aura of toughness, probably useful in this place. He wanted to order a stiff drink, but he thought better of it and ordered a plain cola.

"I'm looking for a girl." He said to her, after paying for the drink.

"Well, you're a good looking guy, you shouldn't have any trouble, honey." She said with a grin, giving him a wink.

Nick smiled, thinking about how his appearance had changed with just a haircut and a shave. It even made him feel better about himself.

"Thanks, but I'm looking for someone specific. Goes by the name of 'Cheyenne'. Do you know her?"

"Yeah, I know her—she's right up there honey." She said, pointing to the band on the stage.

Nick set his drink on the bar and turned around. Through the crowd at the edge of the dance floor, he caught a glimpse of Cheyenne singing on stage. It was the Pat Benatar song, "All Fired Up."

He smiled in amazement at her talent and moved closer to get a better look. Just then he felt someone bump his arm hard. He turned to see a short, stocky bald man with a dark goatee.

"Hey," the man said, "watch yourself!"

"Sorry." Nick said politely. He noticed the man was swaying, like he was drunk.

"Damn right you're sorry! Me and my brother, we're the toughest guys in our town!" The man slurred his words with drunken pride.

"Really?" Nick asked, trying to politely ignore him. His attention turned back to getting a better look at Cheyenne singing on the stage.

*"Now I believe there comes a time*
*When everything just falls in line*
*We live and learn from our mistakes*
*The deepest cuts are healed by fate"*

Nick felt another heavy tapping on his arm. It was the drunk again.

"That's right." the man insisted, pounding his chest with his right fist. "What do you think of that?"

Drunks annoyed Nick, especially ones who thought they were tough. So, turning back to the man, he said matter-of-factly, "I think maybe you and your brother should move to a bigger town."

That was enough to anger the man. He immediately lowered his head and dove at Nick's waist. But Nick stepped back with his right foot, and guided the man past him with his left hand, sending him into some other patrons and eventually to the floor.

Embarrassed, the man got up again and ran at Nick with a rage. This time Nick was unable to escape the man's arm. So he grabbed ahold of the man's head and held it under his left arm. However, the inertia of the man's weight sent him back several feet against the wall. Hitting the wall sent jolts of pain through Nick's already sore ribs. He began choking the drunk while the pain throbbed in his ribs. Then he delivered a strong knee to the man's stomach. When the man rose up, Nick punched him hard, squarely on the jaw. The blow knocked the man to the floor, giving Nick time to catch his breath.

"Stop it!" He heard a woman yell. It was Cheyenne. She came out of the crowd who had gathered around them, watching the two men fight. Nick leaned back against the wall, still hurting. He watched, as the bartender seemed to be escorting his opponent out of the bar.

"What are you doing?" Cheyenne asked, as she approached him with a look of concern on her face.

"Just getting acquainted with some of the locals." Nick quipped, trying to be funny.

"Let's get you to a table." She said, sliding her arm around his waist to help him walk. Finding an empty table, she helped him ease into a chair.

Cheyenne looked at him sympathetically, "I get off after the next set. Try to just sit here and stay out of trouble."

"Okay," he said, wincing and holding his ribs.

She just shook her head and rolled her eyes, smiling as she walked back to the stage. She couldn't help but be intrigued by Nick.

After her last set, she came back to the table and sat down. The crowd was starting to thin out, now that the music was over.

"How's the ribs?"

Nick rubbed his side, "Sore. They said I cracked a couple of 'em."

"Hmm." She said, appearing to be thinking about something. When the waitress came over, she ordered a cola. Cheyenne seemed surprised when she noticed that Nick wasn't drinking alcohol. "What, no booze?" She asked.

"Not tonight," he said. "What about you?"

"I don't drink. I'm a substance abuse counselor and I have this horrible thing about practicing what I preach." She said playfully.

"That's interesting." Nick said. "Counselor by day, Rocker by night?"

"Something like that," she said, smiling. "Which do you prefer?

Nick thought about the question and smiled, "I like Classic Rock, but there are times I could use some counseling too."

"Yeah?" her eyes sparkled. "So, which are you here for?"

"Uh, well, neither actually," Nick paused, remembering his purpose. "I just wanted to say thanks. You probably saved my life out there. If there's anything I can do for you."

Cheyenne cocked her head to the side and squinted at him slightly, "Anything?" Her expression became very intense, like she had something very specific in mind.

"Anything within reason." Nick quickly qualified his words while still being rather curious. He felt indebted to her, but hoped she wouldn't be asking for too much. He already had a full plate.

She smiled and nodded her head, "Okay, let me think about it."

"Sure," he said, starting to feel leery about his offer. However, he did have an obligation to her.

She quickly changed the subject before he could press her more, "So, tell me your story Nick. Who are you, and what were you doing out there?"

Trying to consider how much to tell her, he began, "Well, I grew up around here, and I joined the Marines right after high school. But I moved away after I got out. I was living in Alaska up until a few months ago when I quit my job, and I've been just kind of traveling around ever since."

She contemplated his words and then asked, "Got a wife? Kids?"

"No," he said, shaking his head. "I'm single."

"Haven't found your soul mate yet?" She pressed with a slight grin.

"No," he said. "What about you? Have you found yours?"

"Nope. Still searchin'." She admitted.

He looked her in the eyes with curiosity, "You really believe in that stuff? Soulmates?"

"Mmm… I don't know. It depends on if I find mine or not." She chuckled.

They sat there in awkward silence for a moment. The conversation was making them both feel self-conscious.

Changing the topic Cheyenne looked at him intently and asked, "So, Alaska, huh? I had some friends that took a cruise up there. They said it was beautiful."

"It is," he agreed.

"Is it cold?" Cheyenne didn't like the cold.

"Parts of it can be very cold."

She was curious now, "Where did you live?"

Thinking about it, he said, "Well, I've lived all over the state. But mostly in Anchorage."

"And what were you doing in Alaska?"

Nick looked to see her reaction as he said, "I was a Trooper, then a Correctional Officer." He was usually more elusive with most people about his work, but for some reason, he felt at ease with her.

She wondered out loud, "That must have been difficult work," then thinking to herself how interesting he was.

"It's not for everybody," he agreed as he repositioned himself in his chair, nursing his ribs.

Hesitantly she asked, "So, what do you do for money?"

"Mmm... I've got some investments," he said, being as vague as possible.

She thought about it, and then asked, "And what were you doing out there in the Superstitions?"

"Just out four-wheeling," he said, not wanting to be specific.

Unconvinced she squinted her eyes and said, "Uh huh."

"So, what about you?" He shot back at her hoping to change the subject.

"Me?"

"Yeah. What's your story? Where are you from?"

"Northern California—the Bay area, actually."

"And what brought you here?" He said encouraging her to tell him more. He was always uncomfortable talking about himself, unlike many people who loved to tell their story.

"I came here after College. I don't know... I guess I always wanted to come to the Southwest and learn the Native American way of life. Living in harmony with nature, as opposed to trying to dominate it—that's always resonated with me."

Nick nodded his head, enjoying her reflections.

"It's weird," she continued. "I remember coming to Arizona when I was twelve, with my friend and her parents. I remember driving through Sedona and just feeling so connected and at peace. I promised myself right then and there that one day I would come back to Arizona to live."

"Hmm," He wondered, "Are you part Indian?"

"Part," she said with a gleam of pride. "What about you?"

"Yeah, part Indian, Mexican, Spanish, take your pick—one of my grandmothers was Apache."

"Were you close with her?" she asked intrigued.

He took a sip of his cola. "Not really."

"That's too bad," she said with disappointment.

"Yeah, she was a good woman, from what I remember of her."

Nick wondered why Cheyenne seemed so interested in his heritage—especially if she was part Indian too. However, he dismissed it—it wasn't that important. Perhaps she just wanted to learn as much as she could about all Indian cultures.

She had been pondering something, and finally made a decision, "All right, I got it!" She exclaimed. She wasn't sure why, but she was going to trust him with something big. "You can go somewhere with me tomorrow afternoon."

"What?"

"That's what you can do for me," she reminded him. "And for yourself," she quickly added.

"Go where?" He said.

"Here..." she said as she pulled out a pen from her purse and wrote down her phone number on a cocktail napkin. She handed it to him, enjoying the look of curiosity on his face. She knew she was putting a lot of faith in him to do this. "Call me in the morning—I'll tell you when and where to meet me," she said with a grin.

Nick gave her a funny look. He had no idea what she might be up to.

"What's the matter? You aren't afraid are you, big guy?" She said smiling.

"No!" Nick said defensively.

"Good! Tomorrow night, you'll be thanking me," she said, still smiling." If all goes well..."

"Huh?" he muttered, wondering what he had gotten himself into.

Cheyenne drove west on a long dirt road. Nick wasn't exactly sure where they were. They had met in Apache Junction and from there Cheyenne was driving them in her truck. The dirt road was going west mostly, out of town. It was a long bumpy drive and each bump sent jolts of pain through Nick's injured ribs.

"Are you gonna tell me where we're going?" Nick pressed Cheyenne. It was already late afternoon, and he had no desire to get lost out here after dark.

"If I told you, it wouldn't be a surprise, now would it?" She said smiling.

Nick's ribs were really starting to ache, "Well, can you at least tell me how much longer it's gonna be?"

Cheyenne glanced at Nick holding his ribs, "It won't be long, big guy," she said sympathetically, realizing the drive was causing him some chest pain. "Try and hang on just a little longer."

They continued down the curvy, dusty dirt road. The terrain was dotted with saguaro cactus. Finally, after driving over a bluff, they came to a clearing with a small wooden house.

"We're here." She announced.

"What's here?" Nick asked.

"This is my friend's place," she answered.

Cheyenne parked the car in front of the house, and they both got out. Nick started walking from the passenger's side to follow Cheyenne and approach the house. But when he got to the front of the truck, something made him freeze in his tracks.

There was an old Indian man coming around the side of the house. Nick recognized him immediately. It was the same old man he had nearly run over on the trail in the Superstitions. The old man had long white hair, and he wore jeans and a red and white flannel shirt. The shirt was open, exposing his white t-shirt underneath. He even wore the same purple headband. But how could that be? Was he just imagining it?

"Hello Richard," Cheyenne said as she walked up to him.

"Hello," he answered in a soft but warm tone, as she gave him a hug.

"This is my friend, Nick, I was telling you about," she said, motioning to him.

Nick was still puzzled, but moved forward to the old man. He stuck out his hand to shake with him, but the old man did not return the gesture. Instead, he made a sweeping motion in front of his chest, with his palm down.

"Shap kaij," he said.

"Shap kaij," Nick repeated the greeting back to him. This made the old man smile.

"I'm sorry, but have we met before?" Nick asked, not even sure he wanted to know the answer.

A smile came across the old man's face, "I'm sure you would remember if we had." Cheyenne had a smile on her face too as she saw Nick's puzzlement. She grabbed his hand and started leading them all around to the back of the house.

"We have something special planned for you Nick," she said, then turning to the old man. "Is everything ready?"

"Yes," he said, "my nephews helped me with the firewood. I was just waiting for you before lighting it."

As they came around the corner, Nick saw a large pit filled with firewood. And behind it was a small tent-like structure covered with animal skins.

Motioning to the structure, Cheyenne said, "This is a sweat lodge. Richard has agreed to perform a very sacred ceremony for you." She led him to the edge of the fire pit saying, "You should understand that this is a great honor."

"Well… I *am* honored." Nick said, not really sure of what else to say. "So, what do *I* do?"

"Don't worry," Cheyenne assured him. "Richard will explain everything once we're inside."

"Okay," Nick said as he looked down at the logs in the pit. They were all stacked in a geometrical design. Inside the formation of logs were large stones. Once the fire was lit, it would heat up the rocks. The rocks would then be used in the sweat lodge ceremony.

Turning to Nick, the old man said with a stern voice, "But there is one thing, and it's very important."

Nick felt the old man's intense, serious gaze. "What's that?"

"You cannot tell anyone else about what goes on inside the sweat lodge. It's a sacred ceremony, not meant for outsiders," The old man explained in his soft but firm voice.

"All right." Nick said, still trying to take in all he was being told.

Cheyenne prompted, "You can help Richard start the fire," as she walked towards the old house with her bag. "I have to change clothes."

The fire was roaring by the time she came back. As per Richard's request, Nick had taken off his jeans and blue Henley shirt leaving him in the gym shorts and t-shirt that Cheyenne had previously instructed him to wear.

"It's a good fire." Richard said, seeming pleased.

"Is it?" Nick questioned, not knowing what constituted a 'good fire'.

"Yes, and this is a good sign."

Cheyenne looked at Nick with anticipation, "Well, are you ready?"

"As ready as I'll ever be." He answered.

The old man announced, “Then let’s get started.” Richard lifted the closed flap on the lodge. Bending down, he entered the sweat lodge. Cheyenne had Nick kneel on all fours, next to the opening. Cheyenne could see the look of hesitation on Nick’s face.

“You know, I used to have a real problem with small places,” she said in an effort to console him.

Nick turned and looked up at her, “Really?” He looked back in the darkness of the lodge and thought about his own issues with it.

“Yes, but this has helped me to overcome it.” She assured him.

“That’s interesting.” Nick said somewhat distracted. He wanted to tell her about his own issues with claustrophobia, but she quickly crouched on all fours and entered the opening before he could say more.

He followed in behind her and as he entered the lodge, he had an odd feeling. It was the kind of feeling where you are in a new place, or meet a new person and you feel like your life is about to change; yet you don’t really know how. Will it be something good, or bad? And how will it affect you? Nick didn’t know, but he did know that he was ready for a change. And he would face whatever changes came with his new experience.

It was about an hour before they finished. Afterwards, they sat on some chairs around the fire. Nick was staring into it intently. He was trying to understand all that had happened. Cheyenne was the first one to speak.

"How do you feel?"

"Um, I…I don't know," He answered slowly.

"How is your chest?" She asked.

"My chest?" Nick repeated, feeling his ribs. "They're fine. I don't feel any more pain," he said in astonishment. He looked over at Richard, who was now smiling.

"How did you do that?" He asked him.

"If I told you, you would still not understand. Not now anyway." the old man said cryptically.

"Did you have a vision? "Cheyenne asked, looking at him intently.

"Yes, I think I did."

"Do you want to tell us about it?"

Nick wasn't sure how much he wanted to share with them. He had seen himself frolicking in the water with an Indian girl; plus visions of a mountain and more Indians. He also thought he saw Richard. He was worried that maybe they would think he was crazy; or like someone who was pretending to have a supernatural experience. He mulled it over before deciding that he just had to share something, or it would drive him crazy.

Finally he said hesitantly, "I was with an Indian girl,"

"An Indian girl?" Cheyenne asked, intrigued. "Someone you know?"

Nick closed his eyes trying to remember his vision. "I couldn't make out her face, but it was the way she was dressed," Nick opened his eyes and turned to the old man. "And you, Richard—I saw you. Are you sure we haven't met before?"

With a twinkle in his eye, Richard softly spoke, "What does your heart tell you?"

"I don't know," Nick said as he began to study Richard's face. The old man seemed to know much more than he was telling.

"It's not unusual to feel connected to everything around you. Especially the first time you do a sweat," Cheyenne said reassuringly, trying to make him more comfortable. She knew he had just gone through a lot, and she didn't want to give him too much to digest.

"I will be back." Richard said, as he got up and walked to the house. Cheyenne soon followed.

When they returned, they had plates of food and water. Nick didn't realize how hungry he was until he saw the food. It was a thick stew and Indian fry bread. He ate everything on his plate after gulping down some water.

After they all finished eating, Cheyenne excused herself to take the dishes back to the house. This gave Nick a chance to talk to the old Indian alone.

"Could I ask you about something?" Nick said.

"Of course," Richard said in his calm soft voice.

Nick paused then asked, "Are you familiar with the stories of the Superstition Mountains?"

"Yes, I'm familiar.—the sacred mountains of the Apaches," Richard replied.

"Well, I've been thinking about doing some work up there, but some say the mountains are haunted. I'm not afraid of this, but I wonder, if I bring others with me, will they be all right?" Nick measured his words; he wasn't quite sure of how much to reveal.

"You wonder if the Spirits will accept them." Richard said, summarizing Nick's thoughts perfectly.

"Yeah."

Richard paused, giving Nick's question some thought before finally answering. "I think if their hearts and intentions are good, the Spirits will not bother them."

Nick sat quietly in thought about Richard's words. He reflected that what this probably meant was that there was no real way of telling how dangerous it would be until they went back out there. However by then, it might be too late. Nick concluded that he would just have to be as careful as possible.

When Cheyenne returned, all three sat there, mostly in silence. Reflecting on the evening's events, looking at the fire, and then at the stars and full moon. It seemed so peaceful, almost magical.

Cheyenne had been right. Nick was still struggling to understand all that had happened to him. Yet, he was also feeling a strong connection with the universe now. It was a good feeling; one he hadn't had in a long time. And it felt right.

# Chapter 5

## Friendship

It was cold when Nick arrived back in Alaska. But then, that was normal for Anchorage at the end of January. He needed to come back to Alaska. If he was going to do this, he was going to need some help, as well as people he could trust. Besides, he had some unfinished business to take care of.

It was early evening when he got back in town. His first stop was at the dōjō, to drop off his bags. His business partner, Master Kisae, was teaching an evening class.

Nick and Master Kisae had formed their school of Kyokushin Karate together but Nick had turned everything over to him.

Master Kisae had come to Anchorage and taught classes in his cousin's basement. Nick had been his best student and he was the one who convinced Master Kisae to become partners and open the dōjō. So, when Nick left Alaska, he felt obligated to hand it over to him.

It wasn't as if this was a huge financial sacrifice since the school wasn't very profitable. More interested in the art, they didn't charge their students enough to make a killing, however, it did make just enough to cover their expenses.

Nick dropped his bags at the front door and went inside. Master Kisae was at the front of a class of advanced students and he noticed Nick in the entryway. As soon as Nick entered the dōjō, he bowed to the instructor, as was customary. Master Kisae returned the bow and excused himself momentarily from the class. He walked over to greet his old friend.

"So, you have returned?" Master Kisae said, bowing again informally.

This time it was Nick who returned the bow, "Yes, for a while anyway."

Nick didn't want to keep him from the students, so they kept their greeting brief. They would have time to catch up later.

After confirming that his old room was still vacant, he grabbed his bags and went back outside. He took them around to the side of the building and up the stairs to the two-bedroom apartment, above the studio. Leaving his bags in the room, he called a cab. He could get settled later. Right now, there were some other people he was eager to catch-up with.

The next person Nick wanted to see was his friend, Jim Malloy. Jim owned a successful restaurant and bar in Anchorage called Humpy's. Jim was a successful businessman now, but Nick had known him when he was just a bartender, struggling to make his rent. Jim was a big guy with dark hair. At six foot, and about 200 pounds, Jim was almost as big as Nick, which led to many good-natured wrestling matches. Jim wasn't a trained fighter, but he was a pretty good athlete.

In fact, Jim's father had been an avid bow hunter who taught Jim everything he knew about it. Jim had become quite a marksman with a bow but he wasn't a hunter like his dad. Jim didn't enjoy the killing like most hunters. It was those kind of contradictions that made his friend interesting.

Nick and Jim had become fast friends; sharing an eye for girls, and a love of fun times—but that was in the past... before the dark times.

Jim had worked hard to make his restaurant a success. Humpy's was famous for their many beers on tap. They had loyal customers who enjoyed their good food, and good prices. Situated in downtown Anchorage, it made locals and tourists feel at home.

When Nick walked in, he saw Jim behind the bar. As usual Jim had an audience and was telling one of his stories. Nick also saw something else; a bulletin board on the wall, with a picture from the Daytona Tribune of Nick and his boat crew holding up the gold coins. It was the same picture agent Goldberg had shown him. This meant that they all knew about it too.

Jim saw Nick and acknowledged him with a smile and a nod of his head, but he was just beginning to tell a story, so the greeting would have to wait. Nick stood off to the side of the bar, listening as his friend started his story.

"So, here I am, in the nicest shirt and tie I owned, going to this job interview. Now remember, I'm just a college kid," Jim qualified. "So, I'm walking down the street, and out of the corner of my eye, I spot this beautiful girl walking down the sidewalk on the other side of the street."

"Wait, you spot a beautiful girl from the corner of your eye, across the street?" A doubting female patron asks.

"Hey, what can I say?" Jim said, shrugging his shoulders. "I have a radar for pretty girls." Everyone laughed as he continued his story. "So, I see this girl, and now my attention is diverted. So, I keep walking, but my head is turned 'cause I'm checking her out. But I can't walk that way forever, so finally I turn my head back forward."

Jim paused again for effect. He knew how to tell a funny story.

"Then BAM! Just in time to run into a No Parking sign." The crowd starts roaring at the surprise and Jim continues his tale, "Now, the edge catches me right between the eyes," he said, pointing to the spot with his finger. "So, now I've got this gash in my forehead and it's starting to bleed, I mean bad. Now, I'm out on the street with my best clothes on, and I'm bleeding like crazy. When I finally get to the place, I get some tissues from the receptionist. The bleeding slows down, but I gotta do the whole interview with one hand holding the tissue between my eyes."

This had everyone at the bar laughing. Jim had no problem telling self-deprecating stories, just as long as everyone found them funny.

"That's what you get for ogling that poor girl," one of the ladies taunted.

"Yeah, so what happened to her?" One of the guys asked.

"Never saw her again." Jim confessed. "But hey, it all worked out; I got a date with the receptionist!" He said with a big grin.

Nick waited till the laughter died down before he greeted his old friend. Nick then found a quiet booth and ordered food. It was a late dinner. Jim joined him as soon as he got a chance. Jim wasn't eating, just drinking beer.

"So, what's going on with you?" Jim asked as he shook Nick's hand.

"All kinds of stuff." Nick said calmly, with a half smile. "I guess you heard about Florida." He said nodding at the bulletin board.

"Hell yeah!" Jim replied. "Everyone kept asking me about it. I told 'em I didn't know anything—said you never talked to me about it." Which was true, Nick hadn't really confided in anyone about his time in Florida.

"What about you?" Nick asked. "What've you been up to?"

Jim shook his head "Not much, just working. Business is always slow in the winter."

"And girls? Seeing anybody?"

"Naw, not really, not since me and Michelle broke up," Jim admitted. "What about you?"

Nick shook his head 'no'.

"Any prospects? Anything on the horizon?" Jim pressed.

Nick slightly shrugged. "I don't know."

"Well," Jim said, raising his glass of beer in a toast. "I guess we're both a couple of losers."

They both started laughing at that.

Just then, the waitress came back to the table to check on Nick. Her name was Julie. She was a pretty girl; slim, with long, curly dark hair.

"Can I get you anything else, Nick?" she asked with a big smile, as she picked up his plate.

Returning her smile, Nick replied, "No, I think I'm good," He remembered seeing her before, but she had never smiled at him like that.

"Well, if you need anything, just let me know." Julie said, standing at the table, still smiling.

"Julie, I'll take care of his bill," Jim said after a moment.

"Oh, okay," she said as she broke her smile with Nick to look at Jim. She then turned and quickly walked away.

Nick and Jim looked at each other and started to laugh.

"So, I guess *everyone* knows about Florida." Nick said a bit facetiously.

"Yes, they do."

Nick's face suddenly turned serious as he corrected him, "Well, not really."

Jim now had a puzzled look, "What do you mean?" he asked.

"I mean it's not the big payday everyone obviously thinks it is."

"No?"

"No. In fact, that's why I'm back."

Jim was intrigued, “Why?” he asked.

“Because I’ve got a new deal—a new treasure-hunt. But I need some people.”

Jim looked briefly over his shoulder and spoke quietly, “What is it? What’s the deal?”

Nick gave his friend a condensed version of his deal with Sammy. He did tell him about the Feds, and the Drug dealer. He wanted his friend to be a part of it. And he knew he had to be completely honest about how dangerous it might be.

Jim soaked it all in, weighing each point of Nick’s story in his mind, “Sounds difficult.” he concluded.

“Yeah, and complicated too.” Nick added.

“So, who are you looking to help you?” Jim asked.

Remembering what the old Indian told him about bringing people with ‘good hearts’, Nick also knew it had to be people that he could trust. At this point he wasn’t sure how much of the mystical stuff he believed, but he had enough problems without angering any Indian spirits.

Nick pushed his empty plate to the side and said, “First off, someone I can trust with my life. I don’t need someone getting greedy, or going off the deep-end out there. And second, someone who can take time-off in July. They may need a job to come back to if we don’t find anything.”

“Who do you have so far?” Jim asked. Nick knew he was getting interested.

"Well, I know one guy," Nick said, trying to keep a straight face. "But, he's not very brave, and he's kind of clumsy."

"Yeah?" Jim looked suspicious.

"Yeah, he tends to walk into parking signs," Nick said, struggling to remain serious as he shrugged his shoulders. "'Course, there aren't any parking signs out where we're going, so he might be okay." Nick continued, starting to smile now.

"Real funny." Jim said snidely; then with a serious gaze shot back, "I'm in."

"What?" he asked.

"You heard me, bastard," Jim barked, taking in a big drink of his beer. "I'm in."

Nick wanted to give his friend a chance to back out "You sure?" he asked.

"Hell yeah! I like adventures. It'll be fun."

Remembering some of the good times he and Jim have had, Nick agreed, "Yes it will be."

Jim took on a business tone, "So, what's the next step," he asked.

At this stage Nick was just focusing on getting together the people he needed. "Um, do some planning—see some people." He replied.

Glancing up, Jim noticed some patrons looking for a place to sit down. So they got up and moved to a railing area by the wall. They had to stand, but they could set their drinks on a counter mounted on the wall. Always the good businessman, Jim knew it was better to let new customers have the tables so that they could order dinner. Unfazed by the change of venue, they quickly resumed their conversation.

Jim then asked, "How many people you think we need?"

On the surface Jim might seem like just a fun easygoing guy, but Nick knew he had a sharp mind for details.

"I'm thinking two or three. I figure one of them we should go see soon."

"Sounds good," Jim nodded. "Just let me know when."

"I will. But now, on to the important stuff," Nick said with a smile.

Jim said a bit incredulous, "More important than treasure?"

"Yes, more important than buried treasure." He affirmed.

"What's that?" Jim snickered.

"Jamie. Have you seen her?"

Jim knew full well Nick would eventually get around to asking about her. "Jamie?" he asked, pretending to be surprised.

"I need to talk with her," Nick said.

"Jamie… Now, that's an interesting story…" Jim started. "But first, I have a question."

"Sure, what is it?"

"You still training?" Jim asked playfully.

"Some," Nick said with a grin, knowing where this was leading.

"Good," Jim said as he punched Nick hard, in the arm.

This was part of a ritual tradition of their friendship; punching each other hard in the arm. The punch hurt, but Nick was not about to acknowledge the pain.

They did this all the time and sometimes it could turn into a huge brawl that would usually end up on the ground. People would not know what to make of them. Drinking buddies one minute, punching each other the next. Mind you, this was not just reckless fighting. No, you had to retaliate in a way that would not really injure the other person. And that was a lot harder than people would think. It was more of a show of control and strength than anything else.

"Oh man," Nick said, as he moved his arm around to ease the pain. "We've got a girl in class that hits like that." Nick taunted him. "No… actually, I think she hits a little harder."

Jim smiled now, knowing his friend would retaliate.

Nick held his arm out with a clenched fist to Jim's chest. Quickly, before Jim could block it, he snapped his wrist out, replicating Bruce Lee's 'one-inch punch'. The blow landed hard on Jim's chest and actually drove him back against the wall.

"Now," Nick said, as his friend was recovering. "What about Jamie?"

# CHAPTER 6

## PLAYING WITH FIRE

The sign outside the bar said 'The Penalty Box'. And from what Nick could tell as he walked into the bar, that's just what it was; a rowdy bar that appealed to hockey players and fans alike. The bar was U-shaped, with hard corners. There was a jukebox blasting rock music in front of a small crowd dancing on one side, and people playing pool on the other.

Several people sitting at the bar took notice of Nick when he walked in. He didn't look like a regular—not that it bothered Nick—he was used to it. Besides, he was looking for Jamie.

Jim had shared with him that Jamie's father had recently died and he left her this bar. She didn't have a good relationship with her dad when he was alive—in fact, she was working for Jim when Nick first met her. Now she was the owner of this place and was making a good go of it.

He soon spotted her behind the bar down at one end, serving a customer. Jamie was an attractive girl; about five foot six with shoulder length blonde hair. She had big blue eyes, and a beautiful body. She wore a low cut, blue top that revealed her ample bosom. And her blue jean shorts revealed her firm legs. It might be cold outside, but she could always wear a coat. The tight clothes helped her get tips. Nick quickly remembered why he was so attracted to her. She turned from the customer and was walking towards Nick when she finally looked and realized it was him, standing between the chairs.

Seeing him was enough to make her stop in her tracks with surprise, needing to compose herself. Once she had, she continued towards him, but now the smile on her face turned into a frown.

"I'm still mad at you." She announced to him.

"I know," he said. "But we need to talk."

"We don't have anything to talk about." Jamie said with a firm tone, then her eyes suddenly shifted to something behind Nick.

Nick turned his head to see what she was looking at. It was a guy with long hair and a mustache. He wore jeans and a flannel shirt, and he had a bottle of beer in his right hand. To Nick, he looked like a regular patron.

"Dude, she doesn't want to talk to you." The guy said, grabbing Nick's right arm with his left hand.

Nick was starting to get aggravated—he wasn't here to fight—he just wanted to talk with Jamie. However, now his reflexes kicked-in and he immediately took action to neutralize this guy. With his right arm, he instantly reached around and over the guy's left. Nick's right arm came up under his bicep, locking and lifting it up—effectively putting him in an arm lock. This also kept him from hitting Nick with the beer bottle in his right hand.

"Ahhh! My arm," thc guy cried, standing on his toes trying to alleviate the pain in his arm—but Nick had already casually turned back to face Jamie.

"Just give me a few minutes." Nick pleaded with her. He noticed now another guy sitting on a barstool to his left. The guy set his beer down on the bar and turned his stool to face Nick.

"Now look Mister," the man said, starting to get up.

Nick wasn't in the mood for anymore unsolicited opinions—he didn't have all night to make his case to Jamie. So, he shot out his left hand and grabbed the man by the throat. The man gasped and grabbed Nick's arm with both hands, but he could not break free. Nick's grip was like a vice and he was holding the man firmly, but wasn't actually applying a lot of pressure to the man's throat. That probably scared the man even more, knowing how vulnerable he was in this position.

"Please, talk with me," Nick pleaded, looking back at Jamie once again.

Jamie looked at him, standing there, holding a combative man in each arm as he asked to talk to her. The scene was surreal, almost comical. And he was as cool as could be while he did it. Like it was no big deal—like he did it all the time. That was the man she had fallen in love with—the man who could seemingly do anything.

"Okay!" she shouted. 'I can't refuse him,' she thought.

The scuffle ended quickly with Jamie consoling her ego-deflated protectors with a couple of free drinks. Nick stood at the entryway waiting for Jamie to grab her things so they could go some place quiet.

Jamie left it to her manager to close up and she walked with Nick down 5th Avenue to a café that was open late. They picked a quiet table in the corner. Nick ordered a mocha and Jamie ordered an orange juice—she didn't drink coffee. They sat quietly until after the waitress brought their drinks. They were getting comfortable being around each other again. They hadn't seen each other in almost a year, but still, there was no denying the chemistry between them.

"Jim told me about your dad—I'm really sorry for your loss," Nick said, not sure if she wanted to talk about it or not.

Jamie looked down at her drink, in deep thought. "The cancer hit him right after mom died. At least he's not suffering anymore—he was in pain for a long time." Jamie said somberly.

"I lost my father too." Nick quietly confided.

Jamie reacted in surprise, "I'm sorry," she said sympathetically. "I didn't know."

"Oh, we weren't close—you know how it is." He said minimizing his feelings.

"Still… I guess we've both had some tough times, huh?" she consoled.

He nodded his head in agreement. He started feeling guilty for not being there with her. It couldn't have been easy for her to watch him go through that.

Jamie saw Nick looking at her sympathetically but wanted to change the subject, "So, what did you want to talk about?" She asked getting to the point. She always enjoyed putting him on the spot.

"Well," he started, hesitantly. "I've got your money."

"You do?" she asked, somewhat excitedly.

"Well, not all of it." He continued, struggling for the right words.

She quickly looked crestfallen, "What do you mean?"

"Well, I've got about half of it." He said optimistically, as he reached into his coat pocket and pulled out an envelope. He pushed it across the table to her.

He could see the look of disappointment on her face. "I'm going to get you the other half." He quickly added.

She looked skeptically at him, "Yeah? When?"

"I just need a little time." He posed, "I'm working on another deal."

"Another deal? What about the *last* deal? What about the money from that?" She derided.

"Well, unfortunately there wasn't as much profit from that one as we'd hoped." Nick explained.

"What? I saw the picture of you down in Florida—the one with you and those other guys—and all those gold coins."

"Yeah, I know the one, Nick grumbled. "Seems like everyone's seen that picture. But I'm just telling you, it's not like people think. There wasn't as much money as we thought there would be. But I do have half your money, and I'm going to get you the other half." He reassured her.

"When? I've got a business to run now." She complained.

"I'll have it for you by the fall," he said with a bold confidence. There was a long pause, and then he added with a smile, "Or you can have my first born child."

"He'd be mine anyway." She mocked, smiling. "Why'd you take so long to come back to see me?"

Nick got a crooked smile on his face, "I think it was the, 'I never want to see you again' part the last time I saw you."

Exasperated, she shouted, "We were fighting! Besides, a woman can change her mind." she added playfully.

Nick looked her in the eyes, "Did you?"

She paused and looked him up and down. "Maybe I'm seeing someone now," she taunted, looking for a sign of jealousy on his face.

"Humph, maybe, but he wouldn't be able to replace me." He snickered confidently.

'Ugh, he could be so cocky!' she thought to herself. 'What gall! Coming back to town after all this time, still owing her money—did he expect her to have just waited for him and then to pick-up where they had left off?' Sometimes he just had so much confidence—it was a real turn-on for her. But then there were other things about him that she just didn't understand.

"I missed you," she said, shyly.

"Did you really?" he pressed.

"No." she said tonelessly with a straight face—and then she quickly burst out laughing. She hadn't had a good laugh in a long time. Nick always had a way of making her feel good—even if she didn't know why.

"I bet you did." he said with a sarcastic smile.

They were both smiling now, looking into each other's eyes. The attraction they had for one another was still very powerful—it had always been like that—even when they were fighting.

They continued making small talk for a while, until Nick offered to walk her home. The electricity between them was still strong by the time he walked her to her apartment on 9th Avenue.

When they got to her door, he wasn't sure what to do at first—he wasn't sure about their relationship, but the attraction was too strong. He wanted her, and there was no use denying it.

Softly kissing her good night was all it took. Their desires quickly overtook both of them. They moved from the door to the kitchen—from the kitchen to the living room—until finally they were in her bedroom. They made passionate love, several times. Then in exhaustion—they collapsed in each other's arms. Nick soon fell into a deep sleep. He slept harder than he had in a long time. And he dreamed.

*He was driving down a dirt road in the desert. He came up behind a woman who was walking on the side of the road. As he got closer, he saw that she had long dark hair, and she was dressed in Indian clothing. As he pulled up alongside of her, she turned to look at him. She was an attractive, young girl and she looked at him like she had been waiting for him to come along.*

*"They're waiting for us." She beckoned to him.*

*"Who's waiting for us?" Nick asked. But she didn't answer—instead, she turned and continued walking down the road.*

*"Who's waiting?" He repeated again, and again…*

…until he awoke from his sleep.

# Chapter 7

## Family

Nick was still half asleep when he heard Jamie call to him.

"Listen, I have to go to a staff meeting," she said hurried, as she put on her coat and rushed toward the door. "Call me later?"

Squinting his eyes, he nodded and smiled. She smiled back and quickly closed the door behind her.

He rolled out of bed and dressed quickly—then called a cab to take him back to his place. Once there, he took a shower and had a nice breakfast. He still wanted to talk with Master Kisae, but there would be time later. In the meantime, he had calls to make. There were people he needed to track down.

After a busy day on the phone, it was late afternoon before he could finally meet with his mentor. Nick had changed into his black gi, the karate uniform. His gi had a Tiger—the symbol for Kyokushin—embroider on the back. His frayed, black belt, was tied around his waist. Now, the two men sat facing each other in the lotus position, on the rubber mats."There is so much happening," Nick started. "I don't feel centered. Things have happened to me, and I don't understand it all. In a way, I feel overwhelmed. I've been fighting with people too."

Master Kisae studied the face of his troubled friend and student. "Hmmm. Are there suddenly more hours in the day? More days in the week?"

"No," Nick said, giving the obvious answer.

"Sometimes we wait too long to address things in our lives—we try to ignore them. Until one day, they all cry out to be heard."

"Yes," Nick agreed. "But I have met some people who have different beliefs, different ways. They have shown me amazing things—things I don't understand. They even healed my injuries."

"And their beliefs trouble you?" the master asked.

"Yes," Nick said, realizing it for the first time. "I'm just not sure if I believe in their ways."

"Ha-Ha," Master Kisae laughed and a smile came to his face. "Maybe what is important is that these people believe. Their ways are not strange to them."

"I'm sure they believe." Nick said, starting to understand.

"Then perhaps all you must do is show tolerance. In life, many people have many different beliefs. Is there only one way up a mountain?"

"No," Nick said.

"Then all you need to do is find the right path up the mountain for *you*. Now, tell me, why have you been fighting with people?"

"I don't know," Nick said in a rcsigning tone. "I get aggravated, or impatient with others."

"The self-sufficient man's esteem is not dependent on the opinions of others. Therefore, he is not concerned with their praise or criticisms. Meditate on these things, and try to calm your spirit. It is not good for a man to be in constant conflict." Master Kisae said as he stood up, leaving Nick to his thoughts.

Nick sat there focused on the master's words. He closed his eyes and started taking in slow, deep breaths as he gradually entered a deep meditation for the next thirty minutes. At first he struggled with calming his spirit and letting go all the conflicts he was feeling. Yet, soon he found that place in his mind, where all conflict ceased. Once again he felt one with the universe, connected to all living things. It was similar to the peace he had felt in the sweat lodge.

When the first evening class came in, he was there to greet them. The students seemed genuinely excited to see him, especially his nephew, Darren. He was a young kid, finishing his last year of high school. They greeted each other warmly, but agreed to talk later, as the class was starting.

Master Kisae had Nick lead the class in vigorous stretching and exercises before they trained in specific movements. Later, Nick sparred with his nephew and a few of the other students. Nick toyed with them easily, but he also critiqued them and showed them how to improve their techniques. He loved sharing his knowledge with the students. Just as he had been eager to learn when he was starting, he now was just as eager to teach.

After the class, Nick sat on one of the chairs used by visitors, just off the mats. His nephew sat beside him as they discussed his future. Darren had a short, slight frame compared to Nick. Other than the dark hair and high cheekbones, it would be hard to imagine they were related.

“Mom keeps pushing college, but I don’t want to keep sitting in classes. I want to do what you do Uncle Nick.”

Nick’s brow furrowed, “What *I* do?”

“Yeah, you know, find treasure.” The young boy said excitedly.

“Whoa,” Nick said. “Now, wait. It’s not that easy.”

“But we all saw the picture. Mom was so proud.”

“That’s very nice,” Nick interrupted. “But that picture is very misleading.”

“Huh?” the young man said.

“You see, finding treasure is actually very difficult. The truth is—you know where you *really* go to find treasure?” Nick said, enticing him.

“Where?” Darren asked, eager to know.

“You go to the Library.”

“What?” Darren said discouraged. “Really?” He questioned, in disbelief.

"Yeah, it's true. You have to search manifests, maps, documents, reports—all kinds of boring stuff that, if you're very lucky, will put you on the right path to finding treasure."

"Well," Darren said defiantly. "I don't care; I still want to do it. Please, take me with you next time."

"We'll see," Nick said pacifyingly. "But for now, you need to listen to your mom and prepare for college."

"But I hate the thought of sitting through more classes." Darren protested.

"An important step in life is to overcome the things we don't like, or are afraid of." Nick said.

"Were you ever afraid of anything?" his nephew asked.

"Sure," Nick reassured him.

"Like what?"

"Well," Nick continued. "When I was a kid, I had this terrible fear of closed spaces. It's called 'claustrophobia'. So when I got older, I started challenging myself."

"How?"

"I would make myself stay in a closet. First I did it for a few seconds, then a few minutes. Always increasing the times, until I could do it for an hour, without any discomfort."

"And now closed spaces don't bother you?" Darren asked.

"No, they still bother me," Nick confessed. "I just don't let myself be overcome with fear."

Giving it some thought, "I bet I could do it too!" Darren said. "I bet I could be a good tunnel rat."

"Maybe," Nick pondered. Darren had a small frame, but Nick knew from sparring with him, that he was very quick. "But right now, I think you need to prepare for college."

"All right," Darren said disheartened.

Nick could see the disappointment in his nephew's face. He remembered his own youth, filled with movies of pirates and Vikings, looking for lost treasure—his own childhood dreams of going on adventures to find gold and jewels. He knew many boys had those same dreams—it made him realize how fortunate he was to be living out his dreams. No matter how they turned out—living the adventure was the most important thing.

Nick's thoughts began to drift and he started thinking of all the things he could buy if he *did* find that treasure. He wondered what it would be like to be rich? Perhaps his life would be more at peace and all of his problems would be solved.

For the next few days Nick mulled over his nephew's request before deciding to make him a proposal. After a hard workout in the dōjō, they sat in a local restaurant, eating a light meal. It wasn't until after they had ordered their food, that Nick began the conversation.

"I've been thinking about something."

"What's that?" Darren asked.

"Well, you asked about going on a treasure hunt with me."

The young boy's eyes got big, "Yeah?" he said with great anticipation.

"Well, maybe you *can* go with me."

"Awesome!" Darren said enthusiastically, with a huge smile on his face.

"I said *maybe*. Just as a helper. Someone to clean up, take care of the gear."

"I'll do it, whatever you need Uncle Nick," the boy said.

Nick interrupted his enthusiasm, "Under one condition."

"Sure, anything!" Darren said, undeterred.

"I want you to do some research for me." "Uh, okay." Darren said uneasily. "What kind of research?"

"Remember I told you that you find treasure in the libraries?" Nick reminded him. "Well, I'll give you some things and you do some research for me. You do a good job; I might find a spot for you on my team. Sound like a deal?"

Darren was excited and confident about this proposal, "Sure, Uncle Nick! You just tell me what you need, and I'll get started on it."

Nick's plan for the boy was working. He needed the research, and the boy could use the study habits if he was ever going to make it through college. The boy was so excited; he could hardly eat his dinner. However, after they finished, Nick wrote down some names for him to start researching. The young boy was still excited by the time he got home.

Darren went to the library the next day after school—and the next day—and the day after that. He didn't care how much time it took. He would do the work for the chance to go with his uncle. And after a while, he began to think that this research stuff wasn't so bad—it was actually kind of fun. Like solving a mystery.

# Chapter 8

## Speed

Nick rode in Jim's truck along the Parks Highway, until they came to the Knik-Goose Bay Rd turn off. They were in Wasilla, looking for his friend's house. After driving down a snow covered back road, they found it.

It was an older cabin that sat on about three acres. A couple of chained up dogs started barking as they pulled into the driveway. The long driveway was covered with snow, so they just followed the tire tracks that were already there. There were a couple of out-buildings, with some snowmobiles and four-wheelers scattered around the place. The machines looked to be in excellent condition, a sharp contrast to the old buildings.

After parking the truck at an open area at the end of the driveway, they approached the house.

"You found it!" a voice called out to them. It was a tall, lanky man with long brown hair, coming from one of the out-buildings. He wore jeans and a flannel shirt, with a heavy coat that was open in the front. He was wiping his hands with a rag, like he had been working on something.

"Yeah, it wasn't too difficult." Nick said, stopping to greet his friend. "How ya been Speed?"

“Good dude, how ‘bout yourself?” he said as they shook hands and patted shoulders.

“Hanging in there, “Nick replied. “Speed, this is my friend, Jim Malloy.”

“Pleasure,” Jim said, reaching out to shake the man’s hand.

“Don Sanders, but everyone calls me Speed.”

“Alright,” Jim said, feeling the man’s firm hand shake. “Nickname, I like it. I wish I had a cool nickname.”

“Yeah, I got some names I could think of calling you,” Nick said smiling.

“Shut up,” Jim groused, now regretting his admission.

Speed motioned to the house, “Well, let’s go inside where we can talk.”They walked into the sparsely furnished, one-bedroom cabin. There was a small living room with an old box TV. From the living room, there were stairs leading up to the bedroom in the loft.

Once inside, they sat at the only table drinking coffee. Nick told Jim about how he and Speed had worked together in the past. He also told some funny stories about their experiences at the jail, before Nick got down to business.

“I’ve got a project I’m working on in Arizona.” He started. “I’m looking for some people—people I can trust. It’ll probably take a couple of weeks of your time down there.”

Speed was getting intrigued, “What kind of project?” He asked.

“Gold—a kinda… treasure hunt.” Nick said.

Speed's ears perked up, "How much gold?"

"Enough to make it well worth your time." Nick persuaded.

"If we can locate it." Jim added.

"Yeah, that could be a drawback, if you can't locate it." Speed said, understating the obvious.

Jim continued, "There's more."

Speed snapped his head back to Nick, "More drawbacks?"

"Yeah, we're on a time limit." Nick explained. "It has to be done in the middle of summer, and being that it's in the desert, it gonna be brutally hot."

Speed did a single shake of his head, "Um, I'm not really much for hot weather."

"But that's not the real danger." Jim warned.

Nick looked at Jim then back to Speed, "The area is guarded by Mexican drug dealers."

Speed was surprised, "Drug dealers?"

"Apparently, they like gold too." Nick said, facetiously.

Speed was raised in Alaska. He had never spent any time in the Southwest. Maybe it was a normal thing down there. He liked excitement, that's why he rode his machines so hard, but there were limits.

He paused—looking at them both—with a look of concern, "But you guys are confident... I mean... you're still willing to try it?"

Nick and Jim nodded "Yes" in unison.

Speed got up from the table and poured himself another cup of coffee. "Well, you boys make it sound very enticing." He said sarcastically. "Risking my neck in the desert, to *maybe* find some gold. I don't know, that's prime fishing time up here fellas." He put his cup back on the table and looked at them both.

"We understand." Jim said with a nod.

Speed looked at Jim little confused, "You do?" he asked.

"Sure," Nick interrupted. "It wouldn't be right not to tell you the risks involved. I mean, why risk your neck for gold when you can be safely fishing for salmon on the Kenai River?" He said, in a mocking tone.

"Besides," Jim joined in. "You've got everything you need right here."

Speed looked around his modest home, "Yes I do," he agreed, as the men got up from the table.

"Well, really great seein' ya, Speed." Nick offered.

They shook hands before they all walked outside. Nick and Jim walked to Jim's truck.

Speed walked over to one of his snowmobiles. He put on a helmet, pulled snow-goggles over his eyes, climbed onto it, and kick started it, "Sorry I couldn't help you Nick."

"Hey, don't worry about it." Nick yelled over the roar of the engine. "I'm sure we'll find someone else."

Nick and Jim climbed into the truck and began slowly driving down the long driveway. From the rear mirrors they could see the snowmobile kicking up a huge snow cloud as Speed drove away onto fresh snow.

"Well, that's too bad," Nick said, disappointed. "He could have been a big help. There isn't a machine he can't ride and he really knows his equipment."

"Yeah, seems like a good guy. Any other ideas?" Jim asked as he turned the truck onto the snow-covered road.

"I'm thinking," Nick said.

While he pondered the question, he heard the roar of a snowmobile getting louder and louder as it approached them. They both turned to see the snowmobile angling towards them from an open area to their right. Since the road was covered in snow, Jim was only driving about thirty-five miles an hour. The snowmobile was easily doing twice that speed.

As the truck drove down the road, the trees on the side of the road were getting thicker and thicker. And the banks of the roads were getting higher and higher, until they were as high as the truck. The snowmobile was no longer visible, though they could still hear it. The roar was getting louder and louder, until, it seemed to overtake them, and then, it blasted down from overhead. At the same time, a long, dark shadow crossed over the windshield of the truck. It landed in front of them, setting down perfectly, then quickly sped ahead of them. After getting ahead a safe distance, the machine and rider turned sharply to face the oncoming truck.

Nick and Jim looked at each other in awe at what they had just witnessed.

"Holy shit!" Jim shouted. "I can't believe he did that!"

"I told you, he's good." Nick smiled.

By the time they came up to the snowmobile, Speed had his helmet off. He sat there smiling as the truck approached. He knew it would be a shock to most people that a guy as big as him could make those kind of jumps. He gave the mobile some gas and pulled up next to Nick's window as the truck stopped. He let the engine idle as Nick rolled the window down so they could talk.

"I've been thinking." Speed said, after Nick rolled down his window. "You said it was dangerous?"

"Yeah…" Nick said questioningly.

"Well," Speed said, before spitting snuff on the snow. "I could use some danger. Count me in."

"Great!" Nick said, as the two men smiled at each other.

With that, Speed put his helmet back on, gunned the snowmobile and quickly took off down the road, leaving the idling truck in the wake of his snow cloud. Nick and Jim sat there, looking at each other, thinking about what had just happened.

"Yeah, I think we can use him." Jim chuckled.

# CHAPTER 9

## THE STORYTELLER

It was several weeks later that Darren said he was ready with his information. They met at Nick's sister's house, Shelly.

Shelly was a single mom, who raised Darren on her bookkeeping job for one of the oil companies in Alaska. She had actually come to Alaska before Nick, with her then husband, Michael, who was in construction. However, now she was divorced and struggled to raise her son right. She was determined for him to go to college.

The three of them sat at the kitchen table where Darren had books and papers laying out in front of him from his research. Nick wanted her there so that she could see the work he was making him do. She made coffee before they started.

"So what have you got for me?" Nick asked, after taking a big drink from his coffee cup.

"Well," Darren said shaking his head. "This was quite a project, but I think I was able to piece this story together."

Nick and Shelly looked at him approvingly. He had obviously worked hard on this.

"Okay." He began. "In 1630 the King of Spain was King Phillip IV; a devout Catholic, who was morally opposed to slavery. But, the plantation owners in the Caribbean Islands claimed it was the only way they could make their plantations profitable. He didn't want to upset them since most of them were members of Spain's upper class, and they were bringing in a lot of money for the country."

"So, he allowed it?" Shelly asked.

"Well, he was a King first." Darren said. "This was a man who was raised from childhood to rule a nation. He was obligated to do what was best for his country."

"So, he was conflicted." Nick concluded.

"Yes," Darren said.

"But what does this have to do with my project?" Nick asked.

"Just stay with me," Darren said. "See, at the time, no one knew how large this new land was. What started out as the discovery of a few islands eventually turned into a large landmass, stretching vast distances North and South. His subjects were still sending back reports of new lands. If he allowed slavery in all of these lands, there was no telling how far it would spread."

"So, what did he do?" Shelly asked.

"So, King Phillip decided to halt any settlers from moving into new lands," Darren said. "If he restricted exploration to soldiers and priests, it would be easier to maintain control. Any new exploration would require a license from the government."

"He used the Church to convert the Indians to Christianity," Nick added.

"Well, that proved to be a difficult task," Darren said. "See initially, the Dominicans had been sent over to convert them. But the allegations of rape and mistreatment made the natives mistrust them. It just wasn't working, and as a result, there were many uprisings."

"That seems understandable," Shelly said sarcastically as she sipped her coffee. "So, what did they do?"

"Well," Darren said, getting excited. "The Christian King came up with a new plan. One to help free-up his soldiers from having to oversee the natives at the mines and other operations."

"And the plan?" Nick prompted.

"Right," Darren said, looking through some papers until he found the one he wanted. "Okay, here it is," Darren began reading his notes.

> *"In 1534 Ignatius of Loyola had formed a new Order in the Catholic Church. Earlier in his life, as a soldier, he had been wounded in battle. This brush with death led to a profound religious conversion for him. Professing a vow of poverty, chastity, and obedience to the Pope, he created a new Order called the Society of Jesus whose members were known as Jesuits.*

*He wrote a doctrine called the Spiritual Exercises, which was a missive to show others how to follow the teachings of Jesus Christ by visualizing themselves present at the biblical scene. With his military background, and the member's strict obedience, they referred to themselves as God's Soldiers."*

"Continue," Nick said.

"Okay," Darren said, and then continued reading from his notes.

*"They were highly educated and disciplined compared to other Catholic Orders like the Franciscans and Dominicans. They would be perfect for what King Phillip needed. He wanted the Pope to send them to the New World to watch Spain's holdings. If they could oversee the mining operations, it would free up his soldiers for other duties."*

"And," Darren continued.

*"By freeing up more soldiers, he thought he could stop the incursions of England and Portugal into the New Territories. He believed the Jesuits would be more successful at converting the Native population to Christianity and therefore, could convince them to do God's work freely. And* not *under the bonds of slavery."*

"By God's work," Shelly said. "They meant doing the mining work for the Spaniards."

“That’s right,” Darren said. “So, in 1630 the King made a deal with Pope Urban VIII to send the Jesuits to the New World. A deal that seemed, on the surface, to be beneficial for both the Church and Spain. The Church would get many new converts, and the King could keep his operations going at a fraction of what it cost to have his soldiers run things.”

“You say it seemed to be beneficial on the surface,” Nick said.

“Yeah, uncle Nick,” Darren said. “But the rumor was that by the time the Jesuits were sent to the New World, they had devised their own plan. And, far from the eyes of the King, they would have a continent of new converts to do their bidding.”

“Very interesting,” Shelly said.

“Yes,” Darren said, pulling out some other papers. “But, now the story takes an interesting turn.”

Nick and Shelly looked at each other with anticipation.

“How’s that?” Nick asked.

“Enter Father Eusebio Francisco Kino,” Darren said.

“You see; it was under this scenario that Father Kino arrived in the New World.”

“Father Kino arrives in the New World in 1650,” Darren said, glancing back and forth between them and his notes.

“And who was Father Kino?” Shelly asked, becoming increasingly curious.

"Father Eusebio Francisco Kino," Darren said, reading from his notes.

> *"A mathematician, astronomer, and cartographer. He taught classes for many years before being granted his wish to do missionary work."*

"Interesting," Nick said. "Go on."

"Well," Darren said. "At first, he wanted to be sent to the Orient. But when he got the chance to go to the New World, he jumped on it. He had delays with travel across Europe and issues with his documents. But, he didn't give up. Even though those problems delayed him nearly a year."

"So what happened when he got here?" Shelly asked.

"His first assignment was the Baja. See at the time, the Baja peninsula was thought to be an island. But he led an expedition and reached it by land, which proved everyone wrong. In fact, his superiors were so impressed; they sent him north, to the Sonoran Desert. That's where he really made his mark."

"And where he comes into my treasure story?" Nick asked.

"Yes," Darren agreed. Picking up another piece of paper, he continued reading.

> *"In 1691 he arrived in present day Sonora Mexico. In no time he made great inroads with the Indians. He introduced them to European seeds, herbs and grains. He was a great teacher. His herds of cattle at the Vistas quickly multiplied. His kindness was well received by the Indians, compared to*

*the harsh treatment of the Spanish soldiers. After a while, his value became apparent to both the Spanish soldiers, and the Indians."*

"How was that?" Shelly asked.

"Well," Darren continued. "In 1695, a small rebellion broke out. It seems some angry Pima Indians attacked one of his missions and killed a priest."

"What happened then?" his uncle asked.

"The Spanish sent a young Lieutenant to investigate, and bring those responsible to justice," Darren continued.

"What did he do?" Shelly asked being both curious and pleased with Darren's depth of research.

"This gets interesting," Darren said. "The Lieutenant asked Father Kino for help because he knew Kino was well liked by the Natives. And in a couple of days Kino convinced the Pimas to bring forward someone who had witnessed the attack. So, guess what the young lieutenant did after Father Kino convinced the witness to come forward? Darren paused. "He had him executed."

"What?" Shelly said, looking at Nick in disbelief. "Oh my God!"

"Spanish justice," Darren said flippantly. "That incident sparked an uprising that lasted for months, until finally the army asked for Father Kino's help again. It was only a matter of days before he got both sides to agree to a peace treaty, but the incident was something Kino would never forget. His dealings with the soldiers would be more guarded after that."

"So, the Indians trusted him?" Nick pressed.

"Yes," Darren said, reading from a different piece of paper.

> *"He continued to spread his teachings and build more Missions throughout Arizona, and even into California. He continued his travels and teachings until his death in 1711."*

"Interesting," Nick said. "But what part of his story applies to my project?"

"Yeah," Darren said, looking around until he found the page he was looking for. "Some clues might come from his detractors." He hinted.

Nick was fully engaged now, "Like what?" he asked.

"Well," Darren continued. "There were some who thought he was too sympathetic to the Indians. Some even suggesting he was collaborating with them."

"And…?"

"Well," Darren said, pausing to smile at his uncle. "This is the best part. You see, some wondered how this simple priest, always had the money for the things he needed."

"Yes." Nick said, understanding the meaning of this.

Shelly wasn't seeing the connection, "I don't get it," she said.

Darren explained, "Maybe the Indians showed him where the gold was."

"Or maybe he got them to dig it out for him." Nick added.

"Would they do that?" Shelly asked.

"Sure," Nick said, sharing some of what he already knew. "The Spaniards had the Indians working mines all over the Americas. Usually they did it by slavery. But, maybe Father Kino was able to convince them it was 'God's will' that they do the work."

"Right," Darren agreed. "He was getting money from somewhere."

"At least, we *think* he was," Nick corrected him.

Shelly sipped her coffee, "Well, it certainly adds to the mystery," she said.

Nick nodded slightly upward at Darren, "Anything else?" he asked.

"No," Darren said, shaking his head once. "Kino was the most well known of the Jesuits there, although there were others after him. However, I couldn't find much, and I just haven't had time to research more."

"How much more of the Jesuit's involvement was there?" Nick asked.

"Well," Darren said, looking down at his paper. "The Jesuits were all expelled from the New World in 1767."

Nick slowly nodded approvingly, acknowledging all the work Darren had put into this research. "You did a good job," he smiled.

"Yes," Shelly said, looking at her son with great pride. "I'm impressed."

"Thanks," Darren said, equally proud of his work. "Does this mean I can go with you, Uncle Nick?"

"Well, that's gonna be up to your mother," Nick said slowly, looking at his sister.

She had a frown on her face. "You gonna take care of him?"

"He'll just help out around the camp," Nick assured her.

"Can I, mom?" Darren asked excitedly. "Can I?"

"We'll see," Shelly said, looking at him and then looking at Nick. "But, you still have homework you need to do tonight."

"I know," Darren said as he gathered his things to go to his room. "Talk to her Uncle Nick."

"Okay," Nick said smiling. "Now, get your homework done."

Nick and Shelly continued sitting at the table drinking coffee, as the young boy went to his room. Nick looked around and saw a picture of their mother that was hanging on in the hallway.

"He's a good kid Shell," Nick said. "Mom would've been proud of him."

"I think so," Shelly said. "He wants so much to be like you."

Nick snickered, "He should set his sights a little higher," he said with a smile.

"Oh, mom was always so proud of you too," Shelly reminded him.

Nick thought about his mom, "I suppose," he admitted.

"You know," Shelly said, changing the subject. "I'm sorry I couldn't help you with dad. I know it couldn't have been easy, being with him at the end and all."

"It's okay," Nick said. "I know you couldn't afford to come down there."

"Still," Shelly said sympathetically. "I know it was hard."

"Yeah," Nick agreed. "But, it's mom that I miss the most."

Shelly placed her hand on top of Nick's, "I know," she said.

"She always had words of encouragement for me," Nick said, remembering her. "In good times or bad."

"Yeah, she always seemed to know what to say," Shelly said.

"Pop wasn't too happy when I was starting out," Nick said. "But mom was. I remember, I was having a tough time at the Academy. I told her, I didn't think I fit in, wasn't sure if it was for me."

Shelly seemed surprised, "I didn't know that," she said.

"Yeah, so she tells me, 'son the law has to be equal for everyone'," Nick said, trying to imitate his mother. "She felt that the law needed all types of people to apply it fairly to everyone."

Shelly sipped her coffee. "Hmmm...Too bad those Indians didn't have anyone to apply the laws for them."

"Yeah," Nick said, thinking about it. "Too bad."

# CHAPTER 10

## THE BEAR

The grey bearded hunter loved Alaska. His father had brought the family there when he was just a young boy. If you loved the outdoors, and he did, this was the place to be. He had been fishing and hunting since he was a young man. And now, even in middle age, with a family of his own, he still found time for hunting.

He enjoyed riding his snowmobile on days like today. Up in the mountains behind Hatcher Pass, the air was crisp and cold. With the skies being clear and sunny, he guessed the temperature to be about five degrees. Perfect for a spring bear hunt. But hunting brown bears was nothing to take lightly. That's why he had partnered on this hunt with the two Native brothers. They were both experienced hunters, and good shots.

As soon as they spotted the bear, they stopped a safe distance away. The large brown bear had just recently left his den. His months in hibernation had left him with a huge appetite.

The hunter let the older Native brother, take the first shot. And while the shot appeared to hit him, the bear took off running immediately. He decided to follow him with the brothers trailing behind, that way he could signal them if the bear tried circling back. Bears could be cunning animals.

The bearded hunter rode his snowmobile slowly, looking over the terrain as he went along. Less than a half a mile down the path he saw something, in a small clearing to his right; it was the bear, face down in the snow. Surprisingly, it hadn't gone very far from where it was shot. The hunter stopped his snowmobile about fifty yards away from the animal. "That should be a safe distance," he thought to himself. But he needed his rifle, which was tied down on the back of his snowmobile. He wasn't going to approach the bear without it. So, he shut the engine down, got off, and started unstrapping his rifle.

The whole sequence couldn't have taken more than ten or fifteen seconds. But that's all the time the wounded, angry bear needed to launch his attack. He closed the distance between them in seconds. The bear was on him before he even realized what was happening. The bear swatted him on the back with his powerful paw, knocking him face down to the snow. The razor sharp claws easily cut through his winter coat, and ripped into his skin. The hunter then felt the sharp pain in the back of his neck as the bear bit down on him with its powerful jaws.

Just as the bear started to lift the hunter into the air and shake him like a ragdoll, a shot rang out, echoing from the mountains. The shot tore into the bear's shoulder, causing him to drop the hunter instantly. Another shot went into the bears ribs, which dropped the bear hard onto the snow.

The Native hunters called 9-1-1 and transported their critically injured friend to the nearest roadside where they waited for the ambulance.

Paul Manelli was one of the paramedics on duty in the town of Palmer, when the call of a bear-mauling victim came in. Paul had years of experience as a paramedic, but had only had one other dealings with a mauling victim. However, he knew that all of them were gruesome by nature. Paul made a quick call on his phone as he got into the ambulance with the other two paramedics. It was about a forty-five-minute trip. They had debated flying the patient in by helicopter, but it was decided that they could treat him sooner in the ambulance.

Once the ambulance arrived, the two brothers helped lift their friend onto the stretcher. As Paul expected, there was a lot of blood loss. He spent most of the drive back to Anchorage stopping the bleeding and treating the lacerations, as well as talking to the victim; trying to keep him conscious. The biggest challenge was to keep the victim stable until they got to the hospital.

Providence Regional Hospital is one of the largest hospitals in Anchorage. They have the best Emergency Trauma Center in the state. They were all on alert after they received the call of a bear-mauling victim coming in. They met the paramedics at the doors as the ambulance pulled up into the Emergency Entrance.

Paul gave the nurses the numbers of the last set of vital signs he had taken from the victim as the nurses took the stretcher from him and the other paramedic. The nurses praised Paul and his co-workers for keeping the victim stable before they wheeled the stretcher into the Surgery room. Paul stood there, watching intently as the ER door swung close, reflecting on everything he had done to help the patient and whether it was enough for him to survive.

"Pauly!" he heard someone call out as he passed the waiting area.

"Nick!" he said surprised, as he turned to see his old friend. He didn't recognize the fellow with him.

"Wonder if we could have a word with you?" Nick asked.

Paul looked around at the other people in the he waiting area. "Sure," he said. "On one condition"

"What's that?" Nick asked.

"You buy me lunch."

"Sure thing," Nick said.

They walked down the hallway to the hospital cafeteria. Paul grabbed a tray and picked out his lunch while Nick and Jim had coffee. They picked out a table in a quiet corner and sat down in the plastic chairs. After introductions, Paul told Jim how they had met.

"You see, back in the day, I worked at the jail for DOC too." Paul nodded towards Nick and continued. "Nick here was just a rookie back then. But, he saved my ass."

"How's that?" Jim asked.

"Well, this one night we're booking in this big drunk.

And he's volatile, you know, up and down. Well, I wasn't as careful as I should have been and I turned my back on this guy—big mistake!"

"What happened," Jim asked.

"The guy tries to sucker punch me," Paul said. "And he would have, if it hadn't of been for Nick here. He took him down before he could hit me. He saved my ass that night for sure."

Nick shrugged his shoulders, and said with a straight face "Yeah, but that was before I really knew you."

This caused them all to laugh.

"Yeah," Paul continued. "Anyway, I left the Department about a year later."

"You, were always better at treating people," Nick said, and then turned to Jim. "Pauly taught all the Emergency Trauma classes."

"Yeah," Paul agreed. "But enough about the old days. What's going on Nick? I know you're not here for the food," he said, looking around the cafeteria.

"You're right about that!" Nick eagerly agreed.

Nick told him as much as he could about his treasure hunt, and when he was finished, he asked him to join the team. Nick wanted someone with his skills, just as a precaution, in case anyone got hurt.

Paul had listened intently as Nick told his story. When he was finished, he shook his head.

"Well now, that's one hell of a story."

"I think so," Nick said.

"I'll say one thing about you Nicky, you always keep life interesting." Paul said, and then gave out a hearty laugh.

Jim interjected with a smile, "That's what we like about him."

"And you're sure about this?" Paul asked, running his hands through his salt and pepper hair. As a young man, he would have jumped at an opportunity like this. But he was older now, and twenty pounds heavier, with responsibilities.

Nick tilted his head saying, "As sure as I can be about anything without seeing it. But, I have to tell you, there is no guarantee."

Paul balked, "I don't know, Nick. It sounds intriguing, but you know I've got a teenage daughter that needs me. Her mom hasn't been much help, since the divorce."

"I understand, Pauly." Nick condoled. "Just think about it. If there is any way you can do it, I could use a good man."

Paul paused, giving it some thought, "How long would it take; you think?" he asked.

"A few weeks to get acclimated, some training," Nick replied. "Maybe a month, at the most."

Nick could see Paul wrestling with the decision in his mind. "Oh, what the hell!" he finally blurted. "Let me talk to my daughter. If there's anyway, I'll do it; for old times sake," Paul said with a smile.

After shaking their hands and saying goodbye, Paul got up from the table. Nick looked at Jim after Paul left.

Nick turned to Jim, "Well, what do you think?"

"I don't know. He seems kind of shaky," Jim said, holding his hand out straight and then and then making a rocking motion with it. To Jim, the man seemed too old for what they were going to do. At the least, they were going into the desert at the hottest time of the year.

"Trust me, he knows his business…and we're not going to a Church picnic." Nick sensed Jim wasn't impressed with his old friend. However, Paul had two important traits that Nick was looking for right now; skill and loyalty. He needed both in his team members now.

"He seems kind of old for this," Jim worried, wondering if Nick's loyalty to his old friend was clouding his judgment.

"Think of it as experienced," Nick said with a smile.

# Chapter 11

## Whispering Spirits

Cheyenne parked her truck in the driveway of her two-bedroom house. It was getting dark outside. She had been working late again, and she was very tired. She walked in the front door and threw her keys on the coffee table.

After making herself a nice mixed green salad, she went into the living room and sat down on her soft sofa. It felt good to relax. She had been working a lot in the past few weeks. So many of her clients needed help—and she didn't have anything else going on in her life—at least, not right now. It was funny, how much her life had changed since she moved from Northern California. She had long felt that Arizona was where she needed to be—even as a child.

Her instincts were important to her and she always trusted them—even when she didn't understand them—like now. She didn't know what was coming, but could sense it was something big. It was the same way an animal knows instinctively that a storm is coming. From a very early age, Cheyenne could see things that others couldn't—and now she began to feel as if she would need to gather her strength for what was ahead.

As she picked at her salad, she looked around the room. Just below the living room window, was a small table. Cheyenne called it her altar. On the altar were a number of stones—stones that were special to her—each representing traits that she valued; kindness, patience, faith etc. There was a white glass-encased candle to the side. Behind the stones was a foot-high bronze replica of the horse and Indian from the James Earle Fraser's "End of the Trail" statue—with both Indian and horse slumped down—the warrior still holding onto his shield and lance.

To Cheyenne this statue represented the end of one way of life for the Native Americans, and the struggle to make a new way of life—one that was free of the vises like drugs and alcohol of the white man's world. She worked for the State and gave substance abuse counseling to prosecuted teens, and their families. She was expected to do house calls for her clients.

Whenever she would drive onto the reservations in Arizona, Cheyenne was angered by the conditions of the land. It had unpaved roads full of potholes, desolate fields not fit to grow food or trees and tap water full of arsenic from the old mining days, which no one seemed to care about. The schools had outdated computers and broken chairs—there just seemed to be a lack of resources for the natives. Cheyenne looked at her statue and tears weld up in her eyes.

She lit the candle and some sage then waved the smoke over herself to wash the day away. She said some prayers for her clients and went to grab her salad. Just then, Nick entered her mind. She hurriedly went back to her altar and grabbed a pinch of tobacco, prayed for Nick, and put the pinch of tobacco on the smoking sage. She looked up to the ceiling with a confident smile, and then gazed beyond it to what felt like the whole universe. She didn't know why, but she suddenly had this feeling that Nick would be coming back soon.

She reminded herself that she would meditate in front of her altar in the morning and contemplate these things, but for now she was tired. It was almost 9:30, so she finished the remnants of her salad and got ready for bed. It didn't take her long to fall into a deep sleep. It was in her REM state that she had another one of her vivid dreams.

*She lay in her sleeping bag, half awake. She heard their feet hit the rocks, as the two Indians ran down the canyon, under the moonlight, towards her. Cheyenne lay there, just listening. No one else in her camp stirred—they were all fast asleep. The steps were from an Indian man and woman, running toward her. The footsteps grew louder and louder as they came nearer. When the sounds of the steps stopped, she knew they could see the camp. She could feel their gaze as they looked at them in their sleeping bags.*

*"Who are they?" The female asked.*

*"It's okay," she heard the man say. "They're here to help."*

*With that, they turned and continued running down the canyon. Cheyenne looked around from her sleeping bag. There were other people in sleeping bags, scattered around a fire that had long since gone out. There seemed to be a large man in a sleeping bag next to her. She could not make out any faces, but they all seemed to be asleep, as if they hadn't heard the Natives and their conversation.*

Cheyenne woke in her bed to the sound of whispering voices and the faint pounding of a drum. As she cleared her head, the phantom voices and drumming became louder. "Dance with us," they called. The sounds seemed to be emanating from her living room.

'No, no,' Cheyenne thought. 'Not again—I can't do this. I need to sleep. I have to have rest. Leave me alone!' she repeated in her mind, as she drifted back to sleep.

The next morning, she got up, ready to start her day. After drinking her blended breakfast drink, she poured herself some coffee and walked into the living room. Her usual morning routine was to meditate in front of her altar. Cheyenne was getting ready to do the same this morning.

But as she approached the altar, she noticed something unusual. It was the spear on her "End of the Trail" statue. It was out of the warrior's hand, and leaning up against the horse's neck. How could that be, she thought. She hadn't moved it. And no one else had been here—no one that is, except the phantom voices she heard in her dreams.

'How did that happen?' She thought. The voices she had heard were spiritual in nature; this was a physical act. She was no stranger to dealing with the spirit world—and it didn't scare her as it might others. However, this was different—*very* different. A physical manifestation like this rarely—if ever—occurs. This certainly meant something—but what? She recounted the night's events and the vivid dream. 'What was the message they were trying to give me,' she wondered?

That evening she finished work early. Oddly, many of her clients had canceled their appointments, thereby giving Cheyenne exactly the time she needed to go over to see Richard—she wanted his opinion. So, she drove to his house just before sunset.

They sat on his lawn chairs, staring at the fire in the fire pit. Cheyenne told him of the previous night's events—the dream, the voices, and the movement of the spear. Richard listened carefully. When she finished her story, he remained quiet for a while before he spoke.

"How is your friend?" He asked. "The one from Alaska."

"Fine, I guess. I haven't heard from him in a while."

"I think you will," the old Indian said. "I feel that you two will have a journey together."

Cheyenne wondered what he meant. She barely knew Nick. They had met under unusual circumstances, but what sort of journey would they be doing together? As far as she knew, he had gone back to his home in Alaska. Nick was certainly an attractive guy, but he probably had a girlfriend back home—although, she never asked him directly. They flirted, but Nick hadn't really come-on to her like most guys. Now, this prediction made her curious and she wanted to learn more.

"What role do you see me playing in this journey?"

Richard gazed at her intently, "Your friend needs your help," he answered.

"My help?" Cheyenne said, slightly confused. Of all the men she knew, Nick seemed the most self-sufficient. "How could I help him?"

"Your friend does not have your strong faith. He will need encouragement."

"Encouragement for what?" She asked.

The old Indian just looked at her and smiled. Cheyenne knew it was his way of telling her that he was not going to give her a definitive answer. She nodded her head in understanding and turned her gaze towards the fire.

Her instincts had been right—something big was coming—Richard knew it too.

It was just a few nights later as she was sitting on her couch, going over some work notes, when her phone rang.

"Hello?"

"Cheyenne?" the voice asked.

She wasn't quite sure if she recognized the voice, "Yes?" She said hesitantly.

"It's Nick. Am I disturbing you?"

"Oh no, not at all," Cheyenne said cheerfully. "In fact, I

was thinking about you not long ago. Richard asked about you. Is everything alright?"

"Oh yeah. I'm fine. I wanted to talk to you about something that I'm working on and, I was hoping you might be interested in it. Do you have some time?"

"Sure!" she said with anticipation.

"Like I said, I'm working on something and thought of you. I'd like you to join me in it." Nick offered.

"Okay…" she said with a rise in her voice. "You've got my attention."

Nick sounded like he had something big to tell her about. So, Cheyenne braced herself, but there was no way to prepare for the story that she was about to hear.

# Chapter 12

## Defiance

Just south of Superior was the rock quarry belonging to Diego. It was there that he gathered with his men, in the office trailer. They had spent the winter looking for the mine but were still no closer than when they had started two years before. Diego sat behind his large desk thinking. His men sat around the office too, wondering what their boss would come up with next.

"Who was the one, that one that was killed in the crash going over the mountain?" Diego asked his men.

"Uhhh, Montalvo? Montanero?" Juan was trying to think of the name.

"Montana!" Diego said, finally remembering the name. "*Joe* Montana! I remember now. Marco! Look him up on the computer. Maybe we could find someone who knows something about him."

Marco had a computer on his small desk. He entered the name into his search engine. Surprisingly, it came up right away.

"Hey, boss, I found him!" Marco announced proudly.

"You did?" Diego was surprised. "What does it say about him?"

"It says he was one of the greatest football players ever, and won four Super Bowls."

"What?"

Diego got up and came around his desk to see the image on Marco's computer. He could see from the pictures it wasn't the same man. The man had been clever—clever enough not to give his real name.

"That's not him, dammit!" Diego said angrily. "He was making fools of us."

"But patrón, he's dead. He died before he could find anything," Juan said.

"I'm afraid that's not true," said the old man sitting in the corner. He was cleaning his spectacles with a special dark cloth. The desert sand could be so hard on glasses. When he was finished he put his glasses back on. When he looked up, all eyes in the room were on him.

He had just shown up one day—this old Catholic priest. He was handing out Bibles and began telling stories of buried treasure and gold. He claimed to be a church historian. He also told them he had been to the Vatican and, while there, read many stories of gold in the New World. He kept the men entertained with his stories, even if he often forgot specific details. Diego believed it was because he was old. But, he liked having the old man around. It reminded him of the great treasure he was looking for.

"I'm afraid he's quite alive. In fact, I saw him a few days after your encounter."

Diego frowned and quickly turned to Juan, "You told me he was dead."

"His vehicle crashed! No one could have survived that!" Juan said, defensively.

"And where is he now?" Diego asked, peering back at the old man.

"Oh, I'm afraid I don't know that." The old man said nonchalantly. He waited a moment before adding with a smile. "But I do know of someone who may know his whereabouts."

Nick lay in bed, next to Jamie. It was the first part of July—a beautiful summer day in Alaska. He would be leaving soon, and the tension hung over both of them. They had rekindled their romance, but for how long? They had avoided making any strong commitments to each other for months. Jamie was the first to speak about it.

"I suppose you'll be leaving for Arizona soon." Jamie said somberly, sitting up on the edge of the bed and looking out the window at the warm summer day.

Nick stretched his arms, "The plan is to go next week." he said, still a bit groggy.

Jamie turned and stared at Nick intently, "I'm not going to wait for you this time. I can't do it." She said, perturbed.

"It'll only be about a month." he consoled her. He turned on his side to look at her, propping his head and arm on his pillow.

"That's not the point." she chided. Standing up now with her back to Nick, arms folded at her chest.

"Well then, what is the point?" he asked, baffled.

"The point is, your willingness to take off at the drop of a hat—like last time. One month turns into two, then three, then four. Who knows how long it'll be?" She turned to look at him now.

"This won't be like that." he tried to convince her.

Jamie looked at him with intense doubt, "Can you guarantee me that?"

He pause and reluctantly admitted, "No."

"No! you can't!" Jamie harped at him. "And I can't do this anymore."

Nick's eyes got wide, "What do you mean?"

"I mean... I can't do this anymore, Nick," she said, repeating her words with a softer but more serious tone.

Nick grew flustered, "So, now you need more?"

"Maybe I do." She admitted. It had taken a while for her to admit this to herself too. "These treasure hunts—dreams that even you don't understand—I don't get it—and I'm not going to pretend I do."

"It's nothing we can't deal with, Jaim'." Nick said, trying to sound encouraging.

"You can! But I can't!" she said emphatically. "I don't want to wake up one morning to find that you've left me for some reason that even *you* don't understand."

Nick tried explaining, "I only got involved in this deal so that I could pay you back the money I borrowed!"

Jamie threw her arms up, "I wasn't pressuring you for it!" she said frustrated. "No Nick, you did this because it's what you want to do. It's the same thing as before—something comes up, and you want to take off!"

Nick was completely surprised by this, "Is that what you think?"

"Well, isn't it true?"

Nick became somber, "I thought you loved me."

"I *do*... but... I want *all* of you." She insisted.

"You never needed that much before," he said.

"People change," reminded him sharply. "You know how hard it was for me after you left the last time? I can't do it again."

Nick looked at her with regret, "I didn't mean to hurt you."

"I need more now," she said, ignoring his apology and then redoubling her courage. "It's all or nothing, Nick," she demanded.

Nick's heart began to sink, "I... I can't give you that right now..."

"Then we should both end this." She said unwaveringly. Unable to continue looking at Nick, she turned her head and stared out the window. She didn't want him to see her tears.

The words hung in the air, leaving them both in silence as they contemplated the meaning.

# Chapter 13
## The Journey

The five met up at the airport. Nick, Darren, Jim, Speed and Paul. They had luggage for their clothes and ActionPacker™ cargo boxes for their gear. They had spent several months making plans for what they would need.

They made their initial greetings to each other and checked in at the ticket counter. After they went through the screening process, they all sat down together to wait for their flight. They were headed to Phoenix—all except for Nick and Jim. They would catch up with everyone later.

"How you doing Pauly?" Nick asked him, because he seemed rather nervous.

"Oh, I'm okay," he said, unconvincingly. "I just hate flying. But I'll be fine after a few drinks."

Nick looked over at Jim and Speed—they seemed to be smirking. He knew they didn't have much confidence in his friend. However, Paul was a good man and a loyal friend.

When they got on the plane, Nick and Darren sat in the same row—across the isle from Jim and Speed. Paul sat several rows ahead. Nick and Jim had isle seats, so they were able to talk now.

"So, you never told me," Jim said. "How'r things with you and Jamie?"

Nick shook his head slowly, "Not good. She's not happy about me leaving again."

"Oh, she'll wait for you. It's not going to be that long. And besides, you could come back rich."

Nick made a heavy sigh, "Not this time. I think it's over."

After a while, the flight attendants came through the cabin, pushing the beverage cart toward the front to begin beverage service. However, as they passed, Jim stopped one of them. She was a young shorthaired brunette with big eyes.

"Ma'am, I hate to bother you," Jim said politely. "But I wonder if you could do me a favor?"

"Sure!" the young flight attendant said cheerfully. "What is it?"

Jim pointed to Paul, "You see that fellow up there with the grey hair and brown shirt?"

The flight attendant scanned the passengers, "Yes?"

"Well, ma'am, that's my older brother."

Nick listened to the conversation, trying to figure out what was going on. He saw a smile on Speed's face and assumed he must be in on it too.

"Uh huh," she said attentively.

"He's gonna try and buy a drink, but he's on medication, and he's not supposed to have any alcohol."

"Well, we wouldn't want that." She took note. "I'll take care of it."

"Thank you ma'am," Jim said, giving a wink to Speed. "I appreciate it."

The flight attendants rolled the drink cart up to the front of the plane. They served the passengers drinks, working their way from the front to the back. Paul was sitting in an aisle seat in the seventh row. It wasn't long before they got to his row.

Nick watched as the young woman appeared to be taking Paul's order. He couldn't hear what they were saying, but soon she was shaking her head and they seemed to be in a big disagreement.

Nick looked back and forth between the attendant and Paul, and his friends across the aisle. Jim and Speed both had big smiles on their faces watching Paul argue with the young woman. The flight attendant eventually pointed back to Jim, obviously trying to explain her reason for not serving Paul a drink. When she did, Paul turned around to look back at Jim. One didn't have to read lips to know Paul was cussing profusely. Jim and Speed couldn't contain themselves, seeing this, and bust out laughing. Nick had to put his head down to keep from making his laughter so obvious.

Of course, the flight attendant didn't find it nearly so funny. And she gave Jim a long lecture when she worked her way back to their row. And even though he had to apologize profusely, Jim felt the joke had been worth it.

The rest of the flight wasn't nearly as interesting. And when they got to Seattle, Nick and Jim split off to go to Las Vegas, while the rest of the guys caught their flight to Phoenix.

As they stood in line to board the next plane, Jim turn to Nick, "Tell me again why we're flying to Vegas?"

Tapping his ticket on his hand, Nick said, "There's someone we need to try and talk to."

"Try and talk to?" Jim repeated. "What do you mean 'try'?"

"Well, he's kind of reclusive."

Jim had a look of disbelief, "And you didn't set up a meeting or anything?"

"Well, uh, no. I mean, I tried but…" Nick shrugged.

"Great." Jim grunted. "That's just great."

Boulder city sits just south of Las Vegas on Highway 95. After arriving in Las Vegas, they got a room, and rented a vehicle. The next morning, they made the drive south. Trying to follow the directions Nick was given, they got lost several times, trying to find their way along the back roads. There weren't many signs on the old gravel roads they were taking. It was close to 10:00 AM before they got to the fenced property with wrought iron gates.

Nick pulled up in front of the gate with the rental car. Spotting the speaker and camera to the house, Nick shut off the car's engine and got out with Jim. Nick paused for a moment and looked at Jim. He wasn't sure what he was going to say. He would have to play it by ear. 'Oh well,' he thought, as he hit the button. There was a long silence before they heard the speaker click.

"Who are you?" A male voice asked curtly through the speaker.

"My name's Nicholas Rivera." He said. "And this is my friend, Jim Malloy."

When there wasn't an immediate response, Jim said, "I told you—you should have set up a meeting. Then we wouldn't be out here in the middle of nowhere, talking to a fence."

"Patience," Nick hushed.

Eventually, the voice came back through the speaker, "What do you want?"

Nick looked up at the camera, "We're looking for a 'George Rogers'."

After another pause the voice shot back, "Go away!"

Nick was undeterred, "We're associates of Sam McLain."

"Sam McLain?" The voice coming out of the speaker questioned. "I think he still owes me money."

Nick was trying to think quickly of a way to convince him to talk with them. They had come a long way and they really needed his advice. He looked over at Jim, who was frowning. Nick could see that his friend thought they were wasting their time. He knew that Jim had no idea who George Rogers was, and if Nick didn't think of something pretty quick, he never would.

"Well, Sammy didn't mention anything about money but, if you help us, maybe we can help get you any money you're owed." Nick said, trying to reason with the voice behind the speaker."

They were just about to leave, when they heard a loud buzzing. They watched as the Iron Gate opened slowly.

They drove up and over a small hill before they came to the ranch style house. It had a large covered porch in front, with several metal tables and chairs. There were numerous out buildings and a couple of small warehouses. Mostly hidden from the road—and off to the side of the house, there were numerous pieces of heavy equipment—bulldozers, frontend loaders, and excavators. It was quite an operation he had back there.

Nick parked in front of the house in the circular driveway, just as he saw a man coming out the front door. The man wore blue jeans and a light blue work shirt. He had salt and pepper hair, and wore it kind of long, with a matching mustache. It was George Rogers—somewhere in his late forties just as his friend Sammy had described him.

After initial greetings, they sat at a table on the porch. A young girl, whom George introduced as his daughter Kathy, brought them some iced tea. At first they declined as they didn't want to impose any more than they already had—showing up unannounced as they had. However, it was a hot day and George was already meeting with them, so they acquiesced.

"Thank you for meeting with us. I know this was unexpected." Nick said.

"Not really. "George chuckled, with a sly grin. "Sammy told me you might be coming this way. Sorry about how I was earlier—I just have to be careful of who I'm dealing with these days."

Nick and Jim nodded their heads, but George could see the puzzled look on their faces.

"Oh, I'm being watched. I was followed again this morning."

Nick and Jim looked at each other, not knowing if it was true, or if their new friend was just paranoid.

George continued, "See, no one has an instrument like the one I built." he said with pride. "But I keep it in three places—two are hidden, and the other is up here." he said pointing to his head.

Nick slowly nodded, "That makes sense, I guess."

"Did you have trouble finding the place?" George asked knowingly.

"As a matter of fact, yes. "Nick admitted.

"Well, in treasure hunting, location can mean *everything*—and that's what my instrument does, it locates my targets. You see, we're starting to find out that many of these stories of treasure are true but the locations are wrong."

Nick looked intrigued, "Really?"

"Give ya an example; a few years ago, I was hired to do a job in Northern California. Now, the story goes that two strong boxes full of gold were stolen by some bandits off a Wells Fargo stagecoach. The stagecoach was going from the refinery to the mint. Now, the boxes were too heavy for them to get away quickly, so they dumped the wagon and everything else off in this lake. They were gonna come back and get it later. Then they rode off on the horses that were pulling the wagon. Well, the Sheriff caught up with them and told 'em 'If you tell us where the gold is, we won't hang ya.'"

Jim was getting more engaged in the story, "Yeah?"

"So," George continued. "The bandits told 'em where they hid it, in this lake. And, they hung 'em anyway."

George looked at them both with a straight face and said, "That's fair, isn't it?"

Nick and Jim looked at each other astonished but nodded their heads. They looked back at George, who was now smiling.

"Typical treasure story—somebody's wife had a cousin, who knew somebody. They had all kinds of maps too. But couldn't find it… couldn't find it. Then they wanted me to come back again. So, I told 'em, 'before I take your money, I want to search in some other areas around there.' We eventually found their treasure—it was in a lake about six miles away. But it makes good sense. They probably figured they were gonna hang 'em anyway, so good luck!"

Jim shook his head in amazement, "Wow!"

"That was the second one. Another one we found a while back was nine miles away. So again, we're finding that the stories are true, but the locations are wrong. Maybe even that thing with the Lost Dutchman Mine. Because, think about it," George said, contorting his face. "Does a guy really want to tell anyone where it is?"

"How much did they find?" Nick asked.

"Four hundred eighty pounds!"

"What?"

"Four hundred eighty pounds." George repeated slowly. "In gold bars."

Jim's eyes got big, "That's a lot of gold."

"You know, someone asked me how much gold I thought was hidden in the Southwest." George went on. "I told 'em I think there was enough hidden to fund a couple of small countries.

"The Apaches hid most of it. For the reason being, that if the white man came in and found it, they were going to get the short end of the stick. He would use up the resources like water, and game. And the Jesuits, they went all over looking. And so did the Spaniards. I know a guy in Idaho who found a Spanish cannon."

Nick sat back in his chair, "Really?" He found the conversation with George fascinating. He was obviously able to cover a lot of subjects. But Nick had to make sure he was able to get as much information as he could, relative to their project.

"And you think our site has a lot of gold?" Jim asked.

George took a sip of iced tea, "Yeah, but see I'm not sure on yours if it's the 'Jesuit Store House', as I call it, or one of the Peralta mines... or even the Dutchman's mine."

This was new information for Nick, "The store house?" he questioned.

"Yes, you see the Jesuits were..." George struggled to find the right word. "Well, I'll just say it—I was taught by them in school—those suckers were mean! I don't blame the Apaches for being so mean—they got it from the Jesuits. The Jesuits came here and took away the Indian's religion and destroyed any remnants of their culture. But, their gold—well, that part of their religion they kept.

"They would get the Indians to show them where the gold was and get 'em to work the mines. In return, the Jesuits promised them they would go to Heaven. The Indians would get tired of 'em, have an uprising, and run 'em back down to Mexico.

"Before they would leave, the Jesuits would stash the gold in a tunnel and planned to come back for it later. About thirty years would pass and the Jesuits would start the process all over again. This happened over and over again. And each time the Jesuits would add to the 'Store House' before they were run off."

"They were pretty relentless." Jim said.

"Well, you gotta understand," George said. "They didn't have TVs or X-Boxes. They dedicated their life to this stuff. See, man went and got modern—and forgot a lot of stuff that these guys knew how to do.."

"You think?" Nick asked.

"Oh yeah. They would use the charcoal from their fires and change the pH count in the clay. How do you think they dug out those mines?"

"I don't know." Nick was genuinly curious. He looked at Jim, but Jim had no answer either.

"They had the Indians build fires and heat up the rocks," George explained. "They would get them glowing red hot—then they would pour water on them, and the rocks would fracture. They couldn't use gunpowder to blow up the rocks. The gunpowder was too valuable. They needed it to shoot the Indians."

Nick and Jim sat there in silence. George had a lot of knowledge, and they were trying to take it all in. The talk of heating up rocks to fracture them, made Nick remember his dream and the glowing rocks.

"But their real problem," George continued. "Was that they were just too greedy. They didn't want to share with the King and he was suspicious of this. So, they were finally expelled by the King of Spain."

"In 1767." Nick said confidently.

"Yes, 1767. But another interesting thing was… you know what happened to them?"

"What?" Nick asked.

"They were rounded up, taken back. The ones that survived lived out their lives in exile in France. They never made it back for the gold."

"Interesting." Nick pondered. "So, you think ours could be the 'Store House'?"

"I'm not sure," George cocked his head. "Now, on one of them, the numbers are between two to four hundred Indians buried inside the mine. I'm not sure if that's the one you're on or not. I could tell you more if I went back out and reshot it."

Nick was curious about George's process, "Now, that machine—is that what you used on our site?"

"No, on your site I used infrared. Well, it's not really infrared but that's the best way I can describe it—and soil samples. We used to use a lot of soil samples to find trace elements, but now we use rats. We feed them plant life from target rich areas. See, it's a long process—or it has been. We take a plant and put it in an environmental chamber and ash it out, then grind it, put it in a vacuum chamber, then shoot it with infrared spectra, then photograph it.

"Now, I heard about a guy in Oregon, a rancher, who grazed cows over a large anomaly. He finally contacted me—he was finding gold in his cow's shit. Now, I knew what was happening because we do the same thing with rats. We found that feeding them plant life from target areas, we could find elements in their shit. And it was a much faster process."

Nick was incredulous, "Really?"

"Now, it comes back to my original idea—that you can farm gold." George said with a smile.

Nick and Jim couldn't help but to laugh. This was good stuff.

"Now I have much better equipment I can use, but it would be several months before I could come back out, if that's what you want." George looked questioningly.

"That would be nice." Nick nodded. "But, we don't have that much time."

"With my machine now, it's almost impossible to cheat me out of my treasure." George said. "See, I'm a researcher, and that's what these projects allow me to do. I'm working on some things that would blow people's minds."

Nick was very interested in George's research but needed to focus him on his project, "I do have some pictures that I took. I wonder if you might take a look at them, and give me your opinion?"

"Oh? I suppose." George agreed, as he took the photos and started leafing through them. "Now, are these from the petroglyphs on that hill?"

"Yeah, and these are of some that I found on a rock higher up."

George pointed to a spot on one of the photos, “You see the one of the staff?” “Yeah?”

“That’s the symbol for the church’s treasure.” George said smiling.

Nick got excited,“It is?”

“Sure is,” George confirmed. He enjoyed having more knowledge than others.

Jim was still a bit skeptical, “So, you’re sure that it’s gold on our site?”

“It’s gold.” George snickered.

“Wouldn’t be iron, or some other bullshit?”

“When I say it’s gold, it’s gold,” George said with confidence. “When I say it’s bullshit, it’s bullshit.”

They all chuckled excitedly. If all this were true, they would be looking at a large fortune.

# Chapter 14

## Good Prospects

Bringing George back to the subject, Nick asked, "So, you said that the Indians would revolt—run the Jesuits back down to Mexico—and then it would take them years to work their way back up again?"

"Yeah, that's right," George said. "About every thirty years, the Indians would get tired of being mistreated, and they would run 'em back down to Mexico. Then gradually, over a period of time, they would work their way back up north."

Nick scratched the back of his head "Well, how would they know where to return to?"

Jim was thinking the same thing, "Did they make maps?"

"Oh, no." George said, seeing that they were somewhat puzzled. "Have you guys been out to the mountain?"

"No," they both admitted. However, before they went any further, Jim wanted to clear something up in his mind. "Let me get something straight. The petroglyphs and the Mountain are in two different locations. Correct?"

"That's right," George said, nodding his head.

"So," Jim continued. "The petroglyphs showed them what area to go to, and maybe how to get into it. But how did they know which mountain it was?"

"Well, they marked the mountain," George said with a gleem in his eye. "I'm sure you've seen the pictures. But the markings are only visible at certain times of the year."

Nick nodded, "Yeah, we've seen the pictures."

"Well, knowing what to look for, and the area to look in—that's the easy part."

Jim chuckled, "What's the hard part?"

George smiled and said, "Making the signs."

"Making the signs?" Jim repeated.

George let them ponder that for a moment—and then he asked, "Have you ever heard of a Jesuit priest named Father Kino?"

Nick raised his eyebrows as he nodded "yes", but Jim admitted he didn't know who he was.

"Well, Father Kino," George started. "He was very famous in the Southwest during that time. He was very smart, and had a good relationship with the Indians. He got them to do a lot of the hard work."

Jim pressed, "Like what?"

"Like marking the site," George explained. "See, besides doing the backbreaking work of digging out the gold, they got 'em to make symbols on the area too."

This piqued Nick's interest, "What symbols?" he asked. "You mean the petroglyphs?"

"No, no." George waved his hand. "The big cross on the mountain. It's pretty faint in most of the pictures. That's probably why you didn't notice it. It marks the mountain. You've got similar mountains all over the place. But it was pretty ingenious the way they did it—it only shows up at certain times."

"Really?" Jim said, amazed.

"That's right," George went on. "See, what they did was, bring in a different type of soil and planted it on that mountain. And in order for them to do that, one person had to be down at the bottom of the mountain, coordinating hundreds of Indians to get them to put it in just the right spots—all to get something to show up at just the right time of the year. Imagine how hard that must've been. And you'd have to be pretty knowledgeable to do something like that too."

Nick saw what George was getting at, "So, you think Father Kino did that?"

"Well, if anyone could do something like that," George speculated. "Kino could. He was a mathematician, and a cartographer—he made maps."

This made sense to Nick. "Interesting," he said, as they pondered this point. He was already somewhat familiar with Father Kino and his exploits from his own research as well as Darren's.

Jim was contemplating a previous point and finally asked.

"You said they brought in different soil?"

"Yep, our tests indicate that some of the soil there is not indigenous to that location."

"Why would they do that?" Nick wondered.

"To make a sharp color contrast with the rest of the soil," George answered, letting them think about it, as he took a drink of his iced tea.

Nick paused then asked, "And you can help me locate the cross?"

"Oh, I might be able to help you," George said slyly.

"And you're sure this Father Kino had them mining gold?" Jim added.

"I'm sure of it," George said unequivocally. "In 1947 someone came forward with some gold and silver ingots with Kino's name on them. They had been given to an Indian family in Mexico. Later, around 1980, some more gold bars were found that had Jesuit markings. So, it's not a question of *if* they mined gold—it's a question of what did they *do* with the gold."

"Was Father Kino the last Jesuit priest there?" Nick asked.

"No, he wasn't the last—there were a few that came after him. I believe that the last one was a Father Neve—he was there at the expulsion."

Nick squinted, "Do you know anything about him?"

"Nope. The ones that came after Kino kept a pretty low profile. By that time, they were under a lot of suspicion by the King. Until he eventually had them rounded up."

"The whole expulsion thing was pretty mysterious," Nick added.

"Yes it was," George agreed. "The best guess is it happened sometime around 1767. The Spaniards did it very secretively. They did it as quickly and quietly as they could."

Nick rubbed his chin, "You said earlier that there may be bodies buried in there. Father Kino seemed to have a good relationship with the Indians. Do you think that Father Neve might have killed them?"

George shrugged, "Oh, I don't know. I couldn't answer that. Again, the story is part of the legend. Whether the story is true or not, I couldn't say for sure. You won't really find out until you get inside. And if you want to avoid government problems, you better hope that you don't find any bones."

Nick and Jim looked at each other, thinking about what they were attempting. Hopefully, there wouldn't be any bones—or any government problems as far as that goes. Nick didn't need someone like that Goldberg poking his nose around in things.

Jim was thinking in a different direction, "So, let me ask you about something else..."

"Sure."

"Are there any other maps out there? Anything else that might help us?"

"Oh yeah," George said, somewhat facetiously. "The Dutchman supposedly gave some directions to his mine on his death bed. But again, all of these maps seem to be wrong. I tell ya, the most famous map was probably the Clay Tablets."

"Clay Tablets?" Nick asked surprised, after taking another drink of his iced tea. It was hot sitting outside, but he knew he would soon be dealing with greater heat down in Arizona.

"Yeah," George continued. "As the story goes, this guy finds these clay tablets out in the middle of the desert. They have markings all over them. A horse, numbers, and what looks like a trail. Now supposedly, if you can decipher the markings on the tablet, they will lead you to the treasure."

"Have you seen the tablets yourself?" Jim asked.

George nodded his head, "Oh yeah. They got 'em in a real nice museum in Mesa. They're there on display if you ever want to go check 'em out."

"In Mesa? Just south of Phoenix?" Nick asked.

"Yeah," George snickered then added sarcastically, "All in a nice glass display—they're very proud of it."

Nick looked at George knowingly, "But you don't believe it?"

"No, I don't believe it." George said matter-of-factly.

"Why is that?" Jim wondered.

"Well, again, it's been my experience that all of these treasure maps have been wrong. No one has ever found anything based on those tablets. And they're out there for everyone to see."

"Well, maybe no one has ever figured out the code?" Jim speculated.

"Maybe. But… okay, think about this—if you knew where a treasure was buried, would you really need a map to find it?"

Nick and Jim both slowly shook their heads, 'No.'

"No! You wouldn't have any problem remembering where it was," George said, smiling and then tapping his temple. "It would be embedded in your brain."

"Yeah, you're right!" Jim suddenly understood. He imagined finding a gold mine and knew he would just memorize the location.

"Even if you made a map, you certainly wouldn't want to make an accurate one," George said with conviction. "It could fall into the wrong hands and someone might actually find it and take your treasure."

"Well, that makes sense." Jim concluded.

Nick agreed, "Yeah, when you put it like that, it's hard to argue."

George looked at the two men, "There's a reason these things have gone undiscovered. They didn't want anyone to find 'em that they didn't intend to find 'em. If it was easy, these things would have been found a long time ago."

"Yeah, but you've found some of them." Jim pointed out.

George nodded, "Yes, I have. But I don't use maps either. I use science to find my treasures."

"I guess with your imaging equipment and soil samples, you don't really need a map," Nick concluded.

"If I get a story, and the story is true, all I need is to get close. I can find it if it's in the area."

Nick and Jim looked at each other—they both knew this was pretty amazing.

"Oh, I'll tell you another one," George added. "Our friend Sam has been asking me to do some work on the Florida coast."

"Really?" Nick was surprised that Sammy hadn't mentioned it to him.

"Oh yeah, but I don't get too excited about flying over water in a chopper. It'll be cold and damp—not a lot of fun. But the good thing is, there shouldn't be a lot of overburden. So, that can make the interpretations easier."

"Humph," Nick didn't want to cut George off because he found it all so interesting—however, he wanted to get the subject back to the mountain. "Could you take a closer look at the pictures I took? I'd be interested in your opinion."

"Sure! We'll have more room over here," George gestured to his left and he walked them to an office trailer. It was parked off to the side of the house. Inside was one of George's offices. In addition to his desk, there were several tables. Some covered with maps and charts. Most of the furniture looked like it came from the government. Not surprising, since George said he frequented government auctions.

Nick spread out his photos of the petroglyphs on a table where George had maps of their project. George walked over to a filing cabinet and pulled out more pictures and charts of his own. He laid them out on another table for Jim to look at before moving to the table where Nick was laying out his photos.

"Now these were taken from that Canyon?" George asked while studying the photos with a magnifying glass.

Nick turned one of the photos towards George, "Like I said, I took those from a rock face higher up from there. I don't think anyone else had seen them. They're facing away from the others. But the rock surface is flat and smooth."

George put his magnifying glass over the photo Nick had turned, "Which is why they used it," he added.

Nick bent down and squinted at one of the photos, "A lot of it is hard to read, because it's so old."

As Nick and George studied the petroglyphs, Jim was looking over the charts and maps of the area.

George pushed the photo to Nick, pointing to the rock, "Well, this shows the two buttes, the symbol for the trail, and the cross and staff, but unfortunately, I think the piece you need—in the center here—is very faint."

"Piece I need? What do you mean?" Nick asked.

"Well, you have the symbols for the North and South buttes on each end." George traced the symbols with his finger. "Then you have the trail—I can make out what looks to be a cross and a staff—but this other part here is too faded. But, that can be fixed."

"Hey Nick! Look at this!" Jim called out while pointing to a drawing. He was looking at the group of pictures and charts that George had laid out. "Isn't this the mountain?"

Nick walked over to the table. There was a rough, but somewhat detailed drawing of the mountain.

Nick turned back to George, wanting to be sure, "Is this our mountain?"

George walked over to the two men and looked at the drawing that Jim held. "Yes, that's my guestimate of what it looks like, from the instruments and everything else I used."

"And this is the main tunnel, running up to the surface?" Nick pointed to what looked like a crack with a small opening on the side of the mountain.

George tilted his head to look at what Nick was pointing to, "Yes, it's a natural fissure that runs up to the surface." Then George took the drawing and looked at the two men and raised his finger. "Now remember, there is no gold indigenous to that mountain—it was only used because of the fissure running up to the surface, along with the large chamber in the center."

"So…" Nick paused. "I just want to make sure of something."

"Uh-huh."

"There is no gold naturally in that mountain?" Nick asked, making a short swipe with his hands.

"That's correct."

"So... the gold was gathered from other mines, and placed in this mountain?" Nick asked, still a little incredulous. So many of the stories and legends of those mountains say there is an actual gold mine there. So, this was quite the revelation.

"Correct!" George said with a twinkle in his eye. He liked seeing the light go off in the eyes of the two men. "And they probably selected this mountain because it had the natural fissure cropping up to the surface. And it had plenty of room inside to work in."

"Now then, is it likely that they melted it down into gold bars?" Nick wondered.

"Yes, more than likely." George replied.

"So, if you found it, what would be the best way to move it? In your opinion?"

George put the drawing back on the table, "Oh, you want to smelt it down, and just tell people you're mining—that way you don't have to pay taxes or anything until you cash it in, or trade with it."

Jim was still looking through the other charts and drawings on George's table. "What's this?" he asked, pointing to some marking on another one of the drawings.

"That's water."

"Water?" Jim was a little surprised since it was all desert land out there.

"Yes, I believe that water flows though the mountain—probably at certain times of the year. Maybe an aquafer of sorts, filling up certain chambers in the mountain."

"Well, let me ask you something else." Nick said. "Would they make it that difficult for themselves to dig it back out?"

"Oh, *very* difficult." George emphasized. "You know the reason why?"

"Why?" Nick asked.

"For the reason being—not for themselves—but for the Indians who they were going to get to dig it out for 'em."

"So, do you think it could be sealed with that Caliche Clay?" Jim asked.

Nick added, "That's some hard shit, isn't it?" He had heard that Caliche Clay could be as hard as concrete.

"Yeah," George said. "I know a guy in New Mexico that, rather than dig through it, he just tunneled alongside of it—using it like a wall."

"Great." Jim grumbled unenthusiastically.

"But I don't know if that's what you have there. If you have the one with the Indians buried inside, then no. They would have just blown up the entrance, and sealed it up."

Nick turned to Jim and nodded, "Well then, maybe we have a chance."

"But whatever you do, don't dig up any bodies in there." George cautioned. "If you find *one* bone, you'll have so many archeologists and federal agencies come in—they'll shut you down so fast..."

Nick dismissed this. "I don't think that'll be a problem."

George furrowed his brow, "That won't be a problem? And you're not here to hire me? Just what is it you boys are planning to do?"

Nick and Jim were silent for a moment—then Jim finally spoke up gesturing to Nick.

"You should tell him."

Nick hesitated then told George, "We want to try and get into the mountain."

"You mean dig around? See if you can find an opening?" He asked.

"Well, it's a little more urgent than that," Nick started. "See, we're on a timeline. The Army is taking over that land in a few weeks—turning it into an artillery range. But we've got an even bigger problem—there's another group of people looking for it too—men with guns."

George clicked his tongue, "The lure of gold attracts a lot of people."

"It sure does." Nick said, irritated. "And not all of them friendly. What about you—would you be interested in going with us?"

George drew his head back, "Me? Well…I've got a bad back. It's called a yellow streak." he said with a smile.

"I understand." Nick nodded.

"It is risky." Jim agreed.

"But, I might be able to show you fellas a few things. If you can decode these petroglyphs, you might have a chance."

Nick gave a quick nod, "We'd appreciate any help you could give us."

"Well..." George said, pausing for a moment. "I may not be brave, but maybe I can help you come up with a plan, if you're determined to do this."

"We are." Nick said, nodding his head along with Jim.

# Chapter 15

## The Plan

It was early evening when Nick and Jim got back from Las Vegas. Sammy picked them up at the airport in Phoenix, but they refrained from talking business until they got back to the compound. Nick didn't want to have to repeat himself, and he knew there were things the whole team would be interested in.

Everyone would be there, except for Cheyenne. He had called her before leaving Las Vegas to make sure she was still onboard. She was, and seemed very excited about it. He was going to meet her later and he would catch her up on things then.

The meeting was in an office trailer where he and Jim sat around with the others, telling them about their trip. They laughed, telling them about getting lost, driving around trying to find George Roger's place. And then argued about Sammy's poor directions.

Sammy raised his hands and shrugged, "Okay, so I'm not Siri. But, you did find him, didn't you?"

Nick raised his eyebrows and conceded, "Yes we did."

"He's something else." Jim said shaking his head.

Anxious to hear the details, Sammy said, "Well? Well?"

"He's… an interesting character," Nick offered, trying his best to describe him to the others.

"Who is this guy?" Pauly asked

Jim chimed in enthusiastically, "He's like a treasure hunting professor!"

Sammy added, "He uses thermal imagery, satellite interpretations, ground penetrating radar—all kinds of scientific stuff to locate gold deposits."

"And he's good?" Pauly questioned.

"He's the best." Sammy said confidently. "We were lucky to get him. We hired him early in the process. He went out there with a helicopter and this pilot that he works with all the time—they flew all over the place. He took a bunch of soil samples—all kinds of stuff. He said he even located an old Indian camp not far from there."

Darren was impressed, "Wow, he sounds like he knows what he's doing."

"He does," Nick agreed. "But, he's a bit of an eccentric."

"I told you." Sammy said smiling. "But it was worth it to go see him, wasn't it?"

Nick nodded and smiled, "Yes, it was.""And what did he say?" Sammy was getting very anxious.

Nick and Jim looked at each other, "He believes it's there." Jim said.

Then Nick added, "And he gave us a lot of useful information about the mountain."

"He did?" Speed asked.

"Yeah, and maybe a way to crack the code to get inside." Nick replied.

"Maybe crack the code? To get inside?" Speed was starting to realize that getting in the mountain was going to be harder than he thought.

"Yeah," Nick confirmed. "In other words, getting inside the mountain without having to blow the hell out of it." Nick then reminded them. "Getting inside has never been a sure thing."

Pauly was a bit surprised by this; in his mind it was a done-deal. "No?" he questioned.

Nick shook his head, "No." he said. "So this could save us a lot of time. He thinks the key is in those petroglyphs I took pictures of."

This news surprised Speed as well, "I didn't know getting in was such a problem."

"It is." Nick said matter-of-factly. "But think of it this way—if it was easy, someone else would have gotten in there a long time ago."

"Makes sense, I guess." Speed pushed his hair out of his eyes. "But something else has been bothering me."

Nick glanced over at Speed, "What's that?"

"You never said, but how're we gonna deal with those men that ambushed you?"

Nick looked slowly around the room. When he came in, he noticed that Speed and Pauly had their weapons out and were cleaning them. Speed had his .40 caliber he carried in a shoulder holster and Pauly had his .45 caliber on the desk, in a rolled-up waist holster. They all had brought weapons. Out in the desert, a man might need a weapon just to survive from the animals alone. Nick had brought his short handled pump 12-gauge shotgun. Even Jim had brought his compound bow.

All eyes were on him now. His friends had obviously been thinking about this. He was their leader—they looked to him for answers. After all, he had asked them on this adventure—and he felt the burden of responsibility to get everyone through this safely.

"Our best chance against them is speed. Speed and surprise." Nick said. "They don't expect us. We want to get in and out before they know it. That's our best shot."

"But, what if they do find us. What then?" Speed asked.

Sammy looked around the room at the others, nervously. These guys were his last chance to find the treasure. If they backed out now, it would be too late to find anyone else. Especially anyone who knew what they would be up against. He needed Nick to hold his team together.

"We don't want to get into a firefight with these guys." Nick said adamantly while slowly shaking his head and looking around the room. He wasn't trying to insult their courage, but his friends weren't killers. "I can't tell you what to do if someone puts a gun in your face, but I don't wanna kill anyone over money."

Nick had come a long way since his time in the Marine Corps. It took him a long time to put that part of his life behind him. He didn't want his friends to have those kinds of issues.

Jim was nodding, "I agree."

"I don't want to kill anyone over money either. But I will definitely defend myself." Pauly said with conviction.

Nick knew that Pauly could easily take care of himself, "I understand," he assured.

Jim tried to convince the others, "Maybe we can find another way. I mean, we aren't mercenaries."

"Well, there isn't a bullet been made with my name on it!" Speed looked around confidently.

"Maybe, but it's the one addressed 'To Whom This May Concern' that you have to watch out for." Nick reminded them. "Agreed?"

Nick looked around the room, and everyone eventually nodded their heads in agreement.

"Fair enough." Speed agreed. "But, we need to figure out how to deal with them."

"You're right. So, we need to plan this out."

Pauly knew that Nick was not one to just 'wing it', "I take it you've got some ideas?"

"I've thought about it a little." Nick said smiling.

"And?" Speed prodded.

"Cell phones are gonna be virtually useless out there. The mountains and canyons will disrupt the signals. So, it's critical that we plan this out. We're gonna go over things again and again. Until everyone knows what their role is, and what they need to do depending on the situation."

"Just like a military operation! I knew you were the right man for this!" Sammy said excitedly, slapping Nick on the shoulder.

Nick turned to Sammy then back to the group bringing the conversation back to a serious tone, "Like I said, we'll have speed and surprise on our side. And with the information George gave us about the mountain, it might be enough of an edge to pull this thing off."

# Chapter 16

## A Shared Dream

Cheyenne was sitting with Nick in her living room. It was just after sunset and they sat facing each other on her couch—drinking coffee as they discussed the plans for the project.

"Sammy has a place just outside of town—we call it 'the compound'. It's actually an old construction equipment site, but it has some trailers for sleeping and offices that we need—room for us to get ready." Nick told her. "But of course, with you living here you'll probably want to sleep in your own bed."

"You mean, as opposed to sleeping with a bunch of Alpha males?" She chuckled.

"Yeah." He smiled.

Cheyenne crinkled her nose, "I think I'll wait until we're actually out there on the trail."

"And you got your clients taken care of?"

Cheyenne picked up her cell phone and scrolled through it, "I've adjusted my schedule," she said. "I've given them emergency contact numbers if they have a problem. They'll be okay, as long as I'm not gone too long."

"Good. You shouldn't be." He assured her. "Now, I'll need you to come out on the weekends and evenings, as much as possible to prepare with the guys."

"All right," she said hesitantly.

Nick noticed her reluctance, "You sure you're up for this?" He asked, as he studied her face. "You look like there's something bothering you."

"It's not the guys," she said with a slight smile.

"What is it then?"

"It's just that some strange things have been happening lately."

"Like what?" He asked as he looked around the room seeing Native American artwork on the walls and pottery on the shelves. The light from the lamps gave off a golden warm glow.

"I'm pretty intuitive," she said, almost apologizing.

"What do you mean?"

"Well," she said slowly leaning forward with her elbows on her thighs and holding her chin to her folded hands. "I didn't want to tell you too much too soon." She was a bit nervous to share with him what had been going on. The last thing she wanted was to freak him out or have him leave and avoid her altogether.

"I've taken on a lot so far. Try me," He reassured her, taking a sip from his cup.

"I just don't want to scare you." she nervously chuckled.

A small smile came over his face, "You won't scare me. I've seen a lot of unusual things in my life."

She softly cleared her throat—this wasn't something she was used to sharing with others. "Well, sometimes I see orbs." She began squinting her eyes, like she was expecting him to react. When she saw that he was unfazed, she continued. "Ummm, like small celestial lights flashing over people's heads and shoulders when I'm talking with them."

He could see she was sincere and he was intrigued. "How about when you talk to me?" He asked, smiling and wrinkling his brow.

"Almost *every* time I talk with you." She said with a smile.

He didn't know anyone with this ability, so he wanted to know more. "Anything else?" he asked.

She paused, seeming uncomfortable. She briefly put her hands over her mouth then quickly rub her thighs. Sharing all this made her feel vulnerable to ridicule, but she felt an inexplicable trust toward him. "Yeah." She said reluctantly. "Sometimes… I hear… voices. Like… spirits… in the night—calling to me."

His eyes grew wide, "Indian spirits?"

"Yes, I think so," she nodded.

He pondered the meaning of this. He had his own mysteries to unravel as well. "So, what do they want?"

"I don't know really." She leaned back on the couch, feeling more relaxed. She was almost relieved to finally be open with someone about this stuff.

He was intrigued and wanted to know more, "Are they scaring you?" he asked.

"No, they aren't here to harm me. But they have moved objects around in my living room." She said gesturing toward the open room.

This grabbed his attention. "Like what?" He asked as he glanced all around her living room.

"I have a small replica of an Indian on horseback, from the 'Trail of Tears' statue." She pointed to the statue on her altar.

"Yeah?" He had noticed it when he first walked into her home.

"They removed the spear from the Indian's hand one night." She made a gesture like pulling something from her closed fist. "And laid it against his pony."

He furrowed his brow, "What could that mean?"

"I think they just wanted to make sure they got my attention."

"Did they? Get your attention?"

"Oh yeah. Between that and one of the dreams—for sure." She said, remembering how vivid one of her dreams was.

His head quickly turned to her, this caught his attention. He was still trying to understand his own mysterious dreams. Intrigued, he said, "Tell me about the dream."

She could feel his intense interest. "Well," she began, as she kicked off her shoes and folded her leg under her, sitting on it—she was getting comfortable sharing with him. "Some Indians came to me in a dream."

Nick seemed a bit startled. "How many Indians? How many were there?" He asked intently.

She looked at him with wonder. His interest in her dream was beginning to make her curious as well. "There were… two." She said with a perplexed look.

"Two males?"

"No, a male and a female."

"Young or old, Cheyenne?" He asked a bit determined. His heart was speeding up a bit.

"What?" She didn't quite understand the intensity of his questions.

"Were they young or old?" he reiterated.

"Young—like a young couple." She said, now deeply curious. "Why?"

"The two Indians. Did they say anything?" He asked forcefully. He wanted her to answer without over-thinking it.

"Yes, they pointed at us and said we were here to help," She said, almost as a question. Nick's forceful questions were puzzling her.

"Us?" His eyes flashed.

"Yes, you were in the dream too." She said, noticing a look of revelation on his face. She began to understand his curiosity and questions.

He sat back and shook his head slightly in disbelief.

"Have you had a similar dream?" She coaxed.

He didn't answer her—he just looked away—deep in thought.

Certain now that she was on the right path, she exclaimed, "You did, didn't you?"

He held up his hand, "I don't know. It was just a dream."

She sensed they had been sharing in these similar experiences. "Nick, don't you see, there's something going on here. They're trying to tell us something." She stammered.

He didn't really feel comfortable with the notion that these spirits might have an agenda for him. "Tell us what?" He asked, not liking where this was going.

"I'm not sure."

Nick paused and looked somewhat dubious at Cheyenne. "It was just a dream." He said dismissively.

She started to feel frustrated, but also realized that he was probably not as comfortable with spirits as she was. She composed herself and became empathetic. "Maybe they need our help."

He looked puzzled at her. "Help with what?"

She shrugged her shoulders slightly. Then she looked at Nick with a kindness and warmth he had rarely seen. "I don't know. Maybe to fix something?"

"Huh?" This was getting difficult for him to wrap his mind around.

"Maybe to right some wrong that was done to them." She offered, trying to get through to him. She tilted her head looking at him for a response.

Nick shook his head. "I'm just trying to find—"

"Nick, they chose you!" She insisted.

"What?"

"They chose *you*. And you chose us to help you." She said confidently.

Just then, they heard the hoot of an owl, echoing in the quiet darkness just outside her home. Cheyenne looked to the window and then back at Nick. To her utter amazement, she saw a huge orb above his left shoulder. Her eyes grew big as she watched it spin with multicolors. It was like she was looking at an opal stone that moved and shimmered. She knew it was a sign to continue this train of thought. The spirits were guiding her. She also knew she had to be strong and help him understand the importance of this journey.

"This is crazy. I'm just—"

"Is it?" she interrupted, completely focused on him. "Search your heart Nick. You know I'm right."

"I don't know." He lost the conviction in his voice and seemed to slightly surrender.

There was a silence between the two of them for a while—as if both of them were absorbing what had been discussed—what had been introduced to their relationship and with Nick's project.

Cheyenne took a drink of her coffee as she pondered everything. She wondered about what the spirits were guiding them toward as she asked, "Nick, what are you gonna do if we find that treasure?"

He had thought about this a lot. Over and over the question went through his mind—like a strange invader—taking up more and more of his thoughts.

"Well, we'll divide up the shares as agreed. I'll be rich, and so will you. And so will everyone else on the team."

"And then...?" She asked, tilting her head to the right.

"And then... we'll all live happily ever after." He said with a slight shrug. "I don't know what else you want."

"That's it?" She said, somewhat astonished.

"What?"

"Is that all this is to you? Is that why you think they chose you? To make you money."

"Chose me? Look, I'm just a guy—" He searched for the right words.

"I don't think you're *just some guy*, Nick." Cheyenne put her coffee cup down and gazed into his eyes like she was preparing to talk to the inner most depths of his soul. "I think they picked you for a reason. Search your heart, Nick. You know I'm right. Please, don't you see there is more going on here?"

"I don't know," He said, not really wanting to think about what it would mean.

"Just think about it for a while." Cheyenne said with the warmest voice. Nick felt so comfortable around her. Like he could trust her—even when talking about things like gold and spirits. Somehow she made all of this seem normal.

"Okay," He said. "I'll think about it. But in the meantime, we have a lot of work to do."

# Chapter 17

## The Tribe

Jim and Darren were playing a beanbag tossing game called Cornhole when Nick pulled into the compound in his car with Cheyenne.

"You sure you're ready for this?" Nick asked her before they got out of the car.

"Oh, I'm ready. Question is, are they ready for me?" Cheyenne said with a grin.

Nick had wondered how things were going to go, whether Cheyenne would fit in with the rest of the guys. It would be tough for any woman to deal with these guys by herself, but Nick had confidence in her.

They got out of the car and walked over to the guys. Jim noticed her beauty right away.

"Hi! I'm James," he said with a smile and extending his hand.

"Cheyenne," she reciprocated, shaking his hand and nodded her head. Then she held up her finger. "You're the bartender, right?"

"The Bar *owner*." Jim corrected her.

"Uh-huh." Cheyenne said, somewhat dismissively.

"My real name's Jim, but everyone calls me 'Clutch'," he added. "It's my nick name." Jim looked at Nick nervously, not wanting him to make any comments.

Cheyenne got an impish grin and asked, "They call you that because you have some slipped gears?"

"No, no. Because I come *through…*" Jim clairified, trying to coach her. "…in the clutch."

Nick listened to them both, grinning with amusement.

Jim was taken aback by this girl. She was pretty, but she seemed to have a bit of an attitude. Her greeting with Darren was much friendlier.

"Hi there," she said. "I'm Cheyenne."

"Pleased to meet you, ma'am," Darren said politely.

"Where're the other guys?" Nick asked.

"Pauly and Sammy are in the trailer playing cards." Jim said, gesturing to the office trailer. "Speed should be back any time. He left this morning to pick up the equipment."

"Good. The sooner we get started, the better."

Jim wiped his forehead, "Phew! I tell ya, I grew up in Hawaii, but this heat is something else."

"Yeah, but it's a dry heat." Cheyenne snickered.

"Why don't these people just live on the surface of the sun?" Jim said sarcastically.

Cheyenne knew that the desert heat of Arizona could be brutal if you weren't used to it, "You need to keep hydrated." She cautioned. "Drink lots of water. It's likely to be even hotter where we're going."

Jim replied almost under his breath, "Yeah, I need a drink of *something*."

Just then, the sound of a big diesel rumbled into the compound. Speed was driving a big rental truck, and pulling a long trailer behind it. He pulled up alongside of Nick's car before the truck came hissing to a stop. Hearing the truck, and seeing the dust kick up, Pauly and Sammy came outside too.

"You got 'em?" Nick called out as Speed jumped out of the truck.

"I got 'em!" Speed said, grinning. "We're in business buddy. Who's this?" he said, nodding to Cheyenne.

"I'm 'the girl'." Cheyenne said sarcastically.

"Yes you are." Speed agreed emphatically. Looking her over, he extended a hand.

"Cheyenne," she said, smiling as they shook hands.

"The name's Donny, but everyone calls me 'Speed'."

"Well, let's hope you can live up to that name."

After that comment, Speed just gave her a funny look and walked to the back of the truck with the others to unload the equipment. Unlocking the latches, he stopped before he opened the doors.

Nick introduced Cheyenne to Sammy and Pauly as everyone walked around to the back of the trailer.

Speed grabbed the door handles then turned his head over his shoulder to the group, "Get ready to feast your eyes fellas."

Swinging the doors open, they were able to see what he was so excited about. Inside were six brand new four-wheeler ATVs—five Polaris 850s and one Polaris 1000. Plus, parts for modifying them and a small heavy-duty trailer.

Cheyenne squinted at the ATVs, "What are they?"

"These are your tickets to the treasure, people," Speed beamed. "A little slower than dirt bikes, but they'll take less time to learn to ride. And they'll carry all the supplies we'll need."

"These look like they're brand new!" Sammy said a bit surprised. "Do you really need them to be new?" he whined.

"We're gonna need to get in and out quickly." Nick replied cooly.

"Yeah, but do they have to be brand new?"

Speed clicked his tongue, "It'll sure help."

"Yeah." Jim said enthusiastically. "We gotta go out there in style!"

"Style?" Sammy protested. "Well your 'style' is costing me a lot of money. How much did all this cost?"

"Don't get your panties in a bunch. We're the ones risking our necks." Speed reminded him.

"Yeah, unless maybe you wanna do this by yourself?" Jim added. Like the others, he was suspicious of Sammy—even though he was fronting the money.

Nick turned to Sammy, "This is no time to be cheap, Sammy. Not with our equipment. We have a lot riding on all of this going smoothly. And we can't afford to have one of 'em crap out on us in the middle of the desert."

"All right, all right. Just don't damage 'em!" Sammy chided. "Maybe we can resell them when we're done. I can get some of my money back anyway." He grumbled

After they lowered the ramps, Speed and Jim jumped on the two ATVs at the back and started backing them out. But when Jim drove his down the ramp, the front tire slipped off the ramp. The 4-wheeler tilted, throwing him off of it. He tumbled to the ground with the ATV almost falling on top of him. The others came to his rescue and righted the vehicle.

Cheyenne looked down at Jim, who was now lying on his back on the dirt. "Did you say they called you 'Klutz'?" Cheyenne asked, frowning.

"Real funny." Jim sneered. He lay there in pain for a moment before getting up and dusting himself off. Then he finished helping unload the machines.

Speed called to the group, "Hey, I found something else." He walked over to one of two large coolers. He flipped open the lid and quickly flicked a bottle of ice cold beer in the air catching it in his tight grip, showing it to everyone.

"Yeah! Now we're talking!" Jim cheered, reaching his hand out as Speed tossed the beer to him.

As the day progressed, they alternated between drinking beer and riding. They needed to get familiar with the machines and it was awfully hot—that is, everyone but Cheyenne and Sammy. Cheyenne drank water and Sammy didn't ride the 4-wheelers—he saw no need to, he wasn't going on the trek.

They stopped riding after the sun went down. They built a fire in the fire pit, and sat around drinking beers—all except Darren, of course—Nick wouldn't let him drink. And Cheyenne was in the office with Sammy, looking over some maps.

"So what's with the girl?" Speed casually asked Nick.

Nick drew his head back, "What do you mean?"

"Well," Jim interjected, "you break up with one girl, and then bring another one into this. Kind of sudden, isn't it?"

"Fellas, Cheyenne probably saved my life. If she hadn't found me and helped me out in the desert, I don't know if I'd be here now. She's really familiar with the area and she's a rock climber. We can use her skills—and I trust her—like I trust you guys."

The men sat silently for a moment, staring into the fire and sipping their beers. Then Jim asked, "Is she the one you said is in a band?"

"Yeah," Nick said. "She sings in a cover band, and does counseling for drug and alcohol on the reservation."

"Oh great, she'll love us." Jim quipped sarcastically. "No wonder she gave me a hard time."

Nick looked at him smuggly, "I think you can handle it."

Nick waited for more objections, but the guys seemed to be thinking about it. Finally, Speed spoke up.

"She is very pretty." He said, wanting to say something nice. Then he tilted his beer towards Nick, before drinking it.

Jim raised his beer to the fire and said quietly, "Yes she is."

"But," Pauly added, "It's been my experience that it just means she's gonna be a pain in the ass."

Nick, Speed and Jim all started laughing and nodding their heads in agreement.

"What are you gonna do with your share of the gold?" Jim asked Speed, wanting to change the subject.

Speed looked up at him. "Me?" He then paused and a grin grew on his face. "I don't know. Maybe go to a strip club. Have 'em close the doors, run everybody out but me and my friends. And then tell 'em, 'ladies, you're entertaining me and my friends tonight!'"

"That's cool," Jim said with a smile. "But what about the next night?"

"Oh, the next night too! And every night after that probably," he said chuckling. They all laughed and then his tone turned a bit more serious. "Nah, man. I don't know… probably pay some bills, buy some new machines maybe, quit work, tell my boss to shove it. What about you?"

"Invest it." Jim said with conviction. "I'm a small business owner now. But with enough money, I can jump into the big leagues."

They got quiet as Cheyenne and Sammy came out of the office and joined them. The guys were still guarded around Cheyenne, unsure of what to make of her. It was Nick who continued the conversation.

"What about you Pauly? What are you gonna do with your share if we find it?"

"I'll spend it on women, booze and gambling," Pauly said, making an old joke. "The rest I'll probably just blow. What about you?"

"I don't know—buy a new car—travel maybe. I don't have a real job to quit."

"I've been reading about that lost Dutchman fella, Jacob Waltz. If what they say is true, you're gonna be able to buy a whole lot of cars." Pauly said.

"What did you read?" Cheyenne asked.

Pauly looked up at Cheyenne a little surprised by her addressing him. "Seems he left Mexico with his partner," he continued, "and a couple of Mexicans who said they were survivors of the Peralta massacre. They said they could show him where the gold mine was. So, the four of them came back up to the Superstition Mountains—and they found the gold mine—but that's where the story gets murky."

"How's that?" Jim asked.

Pauly took a last sip of his beer and continued, "Well, Waltz came back to Phoenix alone—with high-grade gold ore. Naturally, a lot of folks took notice of this. He told everyone that his partners had sent him to town for more supplies."

"Yeah?" Jim prompted.

"He later claimed that when he got back to the mine, the Indians had killed his partners. But most folks just thought that he killed 'em himself."

"And no one really knows for sure?" Cheyenne asked.

"No... And when he would leave Phoenix, people would follow him to try and find out where the mine was. But he would always lose them, and then return in a few days with more gold."

"That's right." Sammy jumped into the conversation. "And there's no way he could have mined all the gold that he'd had in just a few days on his own. He had to have found someone else's stash—a mine that had already been worked."

Cheyenne wasn't familiar with the story and asked, "What happened to him?"

Pauly tossed his empty beer bottle in a nearby trashcan and grabbed another cold beer from the ice chest—twisting the cap off—taking a sip. "Well, on his death bed," he continued. "He supposedly gave a map to a woman named Julia Thomas, who nursed him while he was ill. Now, everyone said this map described the area around Weaver's Needle."

Speed asked, "Did anyone ever find anything?"

"No." Pauly replied. "If it's there, no one's ever found it using his map.

"Interesting." Speed said.

Cheyenne took the pause in the conversation as an opportunity to make her exit. "Well gang, I'd love to hear more about this but… I gotta get going. I have to work tomorrow."

The group all wished her good night and she nodded to them and turned—starting to walk to her truck. But then suddenly, she remembered that she had left her purse in the office trailer. So, she made a sharp turn and walked back to retrieve it.

The others were now standing around the fire pit with Jim standing next to Nick. Jim had been quiet, listening to the story of the Lost Dutchman. His head was buzzing now from all the beer he had been drinking. "You know what I think?" he finally asked, swaying slightly.

Nick looked over at his friend, who was staring into the fire. He knew he would regret asking, but he did it anyway "*What* do you think?"

"I think… I don't like you." Jim said as he turned and punched Nick hard on the side of the chest.

The blow was hard enough to knock Nick back several feet. Nick clutched his chest and winced from the pain—the blow was right on his fractured ribs. The others watched in amazement. It caught them by surprise and they weren't sure what to do, if anything.

"The chest? The chest?" Nick barked in disbelief as he tried to recover—still holding his chest where he got hit.

"I told you, I don't like you." Jim said with a scowl on his face.

"You know…" Nick retorted, gaining his strength back from the unexpected blow. "You look like someone who likes to play games."

"Sometimes." Jim said, wobbling a bit, and starting to smile.

"That's good!" Nick said as he cracked his neck and limbered up. "Cause I know a game we can play."

"Yeah," Jim chuckled, "what's that?"

"A little game called 'Who's Your Daddy?'"

With that, Nick dove at Jim, taking him to the ground. The two were in a full blown wrestling match in no time.

"Cheyenne, Cheyenne!" Darren yelled, running into the office. "Come quick!"

"What is it? "Cheyenne asked, shocked by the urgency of Darren's voice.

"Uncle Nick and Jim are fighting!"

She looked at him with concern and confusion, "What? Why are they fighting?" She grabbed her purse and quickly followed Darren running out of the office.

"Don't know." he said out of breath. "Jim just said he didn't like Uncle Nick."

Cheyenne and Darren quickly ran to the fire pit to find the others casually watching Nick and Jim grunting and wrestling around on the ground—about twenty feet away.

Cheyenne looked shocked at Speed and asked, "Aren't you going to break this up?"

"Well," Speed said, taking a sip of beer. "I'm not sure what it's about—and I don't like to get in-between two fellas fightin'—they might turn on me. Probably better to just let 'em wear their selves out."

She huffed at him, "Well, if you're not gonna do anything, I will!"

Clutching her purse, Cheyenne stomped over to them.

Nick had worked his way on top of Jim—he seemed to have him in some kind of chokehold. "Now, say it!" Nick shouted. "Who's your daddy?"

Nick knew that his friend would never say it—he was just too proud. Jim pursed his lips and stubbornly shook his head 'no'. Nick didn't blame him—but he clearly had the best position. He was on top of him and could rest easily. He was feeling pretty good. That was, until he felt the blow from a leather purse smash against his face.

Cheyenne had swung her purse hard at Nick with both hands. The blow knocked him off of Jim. "Stop fighting!" She yelled.

"Oow!" Nick said in surprise, while letting go of Jim. "That hurt! What'd you do that for?"

"So you'd stop fighting!" She barked back at him.

"Oh, we weren't really fighting! We were just having a little fun. I didn't hurt him any." He said, rubbing his jaw.

"But you could have." Cheyenne said. "Or he could have hurt you—it's how accidents happen. And we need both of you."

Cheyenne looked at both of them and shook her head disapprovingly before she turned and walked away.

"She's right." Jim said seriously.

"About what?"

"I was just about to make my move—and really hurt you."

"Yeah?" Nick said mockingly. "Sure you were."

"Yeah," Jim said. "If I had my bow..."

Nick smirked and said, "Yeah. And if your grandma had balls, she'd be your grandpa."

# Chapter 18

## The Medicine Wheel

They spent the next few weeks training with the four-wheelers, riding during the day to get familiar with them as well as getting aclimated to the harsh desert heat. Speed was also making modifications to the four-wheelers. He wanted to get as much speed out of them as possible. In the evenings, Nick would go over the plans. Sometimes he would bring them all in to discuss something and other times he would talk to them individually about their roles.

They had three weeks to train before they needed to leave. Nick thought he had given himself, and them, enough time. But no amount of planning can account for the unexpected.

Darren was having difficulty keeping up with the others on the four-wheelers. Even though he wasn't going to be going out on the trail with the others, it was still frustrating to him. Though, it was to be expected since they were more experienced. He was a lot lighter but the lighter weight wasn't enough to overcome their riding skills, especially Speed's. He rode his four-wheeler like a mad man. He certainly lived up to his nickname.

But, on this day, Darren had a new plan—this race would be different. They may have gotten off to a faster start, but he thought he could catch them on the trail. Especially Pauly, he was older and less competitive than the others. He didn't seem to be racing like the others—Pauly just didn't want to come in last. As long as he beat Darren, he was satisfied.

Darren was now gaining ground on him. And just past the next curve, there was a straightaway, with a mound before the next curve. If he could jump that mound, he could leap ahead of Pauly. He would catch him off guard.

As they came into the straightaway, Darren hit the throttle. By the time he reached the mound, he was almost even with Pauly. As he lifted into the air, he still thought his plan would work. Once Pauly saw him, he would have to slow down and let him pass. But, the problem was, Pauly didn't see him. He had started into the turn early. The only thing he saw was the tire of the other four-wheeler coming down on him.

"Nick, come quick. And bring the truck," Jim's voice came over the radio, as Nick sat in the office with Sammy. They were going over expense reports, while the others were out riding. "Pauly's hurt!"

"I'm on my way!" Nick said into his radio as he grabbed the keys. "What's your location?"

"About a quarter mile south of the bridge on the trail." Jim's voice crackled out of the radio.

Nick was out to the truck and driving down the trail in no time. They were using an area adjacent to the construction camp. He was familiar with the bridge, as they had used the same trail to train on many times. It wasn't long before Nick arrived on the scene.

Pauly was lying on a dry creek bed, the others were gathered around him. Cheyenne was giving him water, while Speed and Jim appeared to be tending to his right leg. Nick ran from the truck to his friend.

"Pauly!" Nick called out, "What happened?"

"It's my fault Uncle Nick," Darren said, feeling guilty. "We were racing, and I guess I cut him off."

"His leg is broken," Speed announced. "We need to get him to a hospital, see if there's any more internal damage."

Nick made a quick nod of his head and looked down on his friend.

"Not a Hospital!" Pauly protested, looking up at him with a scowl. "That's where they take people to die."

Even though this was a rather ironic thing for him to say, considering that he was a paramedic and took people to the hospital all the time—Pauly truly hated the idea of being sick in a hospital.

"You're too mean to die," Nick said, looking down on his friend. They both smiled before Nick asked, "What can we do?"

Pauly knew more about emergency care than any of them. That's why Nick wanted him to come along. As long as he was conscious, he could best tell them how to treat him.

"Splint the leg, try to keep me stabilized." Pauly said. "I don't think I've lost much blood. And hey, try not to hit any bumps on the way out, would you?"

Nick was concerned but glad his friend was in good spirits. "Sure, no problem," He said smiling.

They lifted Pauly up and placed him in the bed of the truck. Nick drove carefully, not wanting to jar Pauly any more than he had to. With the rocky trail, before hitting pavement, it made for a long, slow ride to the nearest hospital.

The next day, Nick came to visit. He went to the nurse's station on the third floor.

"I'm here to see Paul Manelli." Nick said.

"Are you a friend or family?" the nurse behind the counter asked.

"Just a friend," Nick said. "He doesn't have any family here."

The nurse typed into the computer, searched the screen and then looked up at Nick with a scowl, saying, "He's in 311—down the hall, to the left."

From the look on the nurse's face, Nick was sure his friend had been giving them problems. Pauly truly hated having to be in a hospital, which made him the epitomy of the 'patient-from-hell' to be around.

Nick stood at the doorway to the room and knocked on the door frame."How you feelin' old man," He said as he walked into the private room.

"Oh hell, little bit of pain," Pauly said with a smile. "But they give me some good drugs."

"Yeah," Nick chuckled. "That's what you need."

"You bet!"

"Darren feels terrible about this—he wanted me to tell you. I think he was too scared to come." Nick said, smiling.

"Oh no. It was an accident. He's not the first kid to drive reckless. I'd hate to tell you all the stupid things I did as a kid."

Nick nodded his head in agreement. "How are you doing, really?"

"I'm all right, Nick. I'm just sorry I won't be able to finish this with you."

Nodding his head Nick said, "So am I! You'll still get your share."

"Nah, I haven't done anything," Pauly said, waving his hand. "But I would appreciate it if you covered my expenses."

"Of course. Have you talked to your family?"

"Yeah, I talked to my daughter. She wanted to come down. I told her not to bother. I'll be back soon enough."

Nick looked out the room window to a sunny sky and distant mountains, then said, "I still wish you were coming."

"Yeah, so do I," Pauly said somewhat apologetically, "but you'll be fine."

"I don't know. I'm not sure if we can finish."

Pauly pulled his head back and said quizically, "What do you mean?"

"Well, I wanted someone who could take care of us if someone got injured. I sure hadn't planned on *you* getting hurt."

Pauly slightly threw up his hands, "Oh hell, this stuff happens."

"Yeah," Nick agreed.

"But you can set a splint as well as anyone if you need to. Besides…" Pauly said with a wink, "if there's a wound and you can't stop the bleeding, you'll be too far from a hospital to do much for them anyway."

Nick furrowed his brow. "Yeah, you're right my friend." He conceded.

"Awww, get out there and find your treasure." Pauly gestured to the door.

Nick said goodbye to his old friend and left the hospital. He wasn't feeling good about this. Maybe this *was* too dangerous. They were lucky Pauly's injuries weren't more severe—and they hadn't even started yet.

Pauly was right—if someone were injured seriously, they'd be a long way away from any hospitals. What would happen if one of his friends got shot? Maybe he was crazy to do this—going after a mythical treasure while trying to elude dangerous gunmen. Was he really that desperate to make money?

He thought about this on the drive back to the compound. Maybe he should just go back to Alaska and get a job. Maybe Jamie would take him back. Did he really want the responsibility if another friend got hurt?

But, on the other hand, what if he found it? It could make him and the others rich beyond their wildest dreams. Money could erase any problems. As the days passed, his thoughts had been turning more and more to what his life would be like if he were rich. Wouldn't it all be worth it to find the gold?

Or, maybe gold fever had gone to his head. Thougthts of treasure can take over a man's mind, until he becomes obsessed with it. Making him take chances he would never normally take. Was that what was driving him now. He needed to think more about it.

# Chapter 19

## Infancy, Youth, Middle & Old Age

Nick drove the rental truck down the gravel road with Cheyenne. He had told her about his doubts about the project now with Pauly off the team. She had been adamant that Nick continued, but he was not so sure. He wasn't sure if it was the feeling of imminent danger or impending failure.

With Pauly gone, he needed Darren to take his position on the team. This wasn't what Nick had planned. Taking his nephew out there made him uncomfortable. If anything happened, Nick would feel responsible.

He had his own intuitive feelings—and he was beginning to feel that something was wrong. Since Cheyenne strongly disagreed, she convinced him that they should go to see Richard—to do a sweat lodge and ask him for guidance.

They drove along the gravel roads, Nick asking her for directions along the way.

"I'm sorry," she said. "I keep thinking you know where you're going."

"That's okay," Nick said with a chuckle. "I keep making that same mistake myself."

They both laughed as they continued on their journey. They reached Richard's house a short time later. He came out of the house to greet them when they pulled up.

"Shap kaij," Richard said, waving his hand out, palm down.

Nick repeated the gesture, as he had been shown. Cheyenne wasted no time in giving her old friend a hug.

"Thanks for seeing me." Nick said.

Richard smiled and said, "Let's go back here and we can talk."

"Sure."

They walked to the back of the house where the sweat lodge was set up. Around the fire pit were some lawn chairs. They sat down and Nick tried to verbalize what he was feeling as well as describing the conflict with Cheyenne. However, now that he was there, he wasn't sure if Richard was going to be impartial about this.

"I don't know how much Cheyenne has told you, so I'll just come out and say it," Nick started, "I'm working on a project, looking for a buried treasure. I'm not exactly sure, but I think it may have been mined by Indians under the direction of Jesuit priests a long, long time ago."

"I have heard stories of our people doing work for the 'Black Robes'—or the Jesuits, as you call them." Richard said in his soft voice.

"Well, anyway," Nick continued. "I'm not sure if I want to go on with it. A good friend of mine got hurt recently—and some very bad men may be watching this place. I don't want to be responsible for anyone else getting hurt. I've been responsible for people before. I'm not sure that I want that again."

"You mean in your work up in Alaska?" Cheyenne asked.

"Yeah," Nick said, "in Alaska."

Cheyenne was listening to him intently. She realized that Nick's regrets weighed heavily on him and she did not want to discredit this. She had empathy for his position. She could also not deny her own visions and feeling of this project. She nodded, looking at him with care. She gently offered, "Nick, I think there is something bigger than all of us, calling you to do this project. I think the spirits want you here, and they want you to do this."

"I'm just a regular guy, trying to make some money. I've never talked to the spirits. Hell, I'd never been in a sweat lodge until I met you." Nick protested.

"I appreciate your humility, but I think you are special—I believe the spirits think you are too. And that's why they want you to do this." Cheyenne insisted and then turning to the old Indian she asked. "What do you think Richard?"

Richard slowly leaned forward in his chair, facing Cheyenne and nodding. "I too think Nick has been called here for a reason," he said. Then turning to Nick he looked at him with an intense gaze and spoke softly, "but let me ask, what would you hope to do with it—if you found a great treasure?"

Richard and Cheyenne were both now staring at Nick. The question was unsettling—he had been thinking about it more and more. He found himself having dreams of buying a new car, or house, or boat—but afterwards, life would still go on. What would others think of him? What else did he want to do? Who did he want to become?

Nick was fidgeting with a small twig, tapping it with one hand on the other. He looked down at it like it was going to give him an answer, and then he quickly tossed it into the fire, watching it ignite and become ash. "I…I don't know," he admitted, looking up at them both.

Richard looked into Nick's eyes for a moment, then he turned away looking all around at the beautiful trees and land. He looked as if he were searching or listening for something. Then he eventually smiled with complete satisfaction and looked at Cheyenne and Nick.

"Let's do a sweat." Richard said, smiling.

The three of them changed their clothes and then entered the sweat lodge. Nick no longer found the sweat lodge odd or strange. It was becoming comfortable for him.

Afterwards, they sat around the fire again. Soon Richard brought out food and tea from the house. They ate the meal, before they started talking again.

"How do you feel now?" Richard asked, setting his empty plate on the ground.

"Much better—like a big weight has been lifted off my shoulders." Nick said, drinking from a big glass of iced tea.

"Why is that?" Richard asked.

Nick paused in deep thought then said, "I don't know. I just feel centered now." He took a long deep breath, like he was breathing fresh air for the first time. "I had another vision while doing the sweat," he confided. "I saw myself in a number of different situations, but whether I was rich, poor, old or young, I was still the same person. Maybe that was the clarity I was looking for."

"That was your vision?" Richard asked with interest.

"Yes." Nick nodded.

"And what were you shown?"

Nick paused again to gather his thoughts, "That no matter my circumstances, I need to remain true to myself," he said, beginning to understand it.

"Wow! Cheyenne said. "It must have been a powerful vision."

Nick nodded calmly, "Yes, it was."

"And you feel better?" She asked, smiling.

Nick sighed, "Much better."

"Good, because I had a vision too." Cheyenne shared.

"You did?"

Cheyenne pulled her leg up, sitting on it, then closed her eyes and reached out her hands gesturing out beyond the fire. "I saw many Indian people asking for our help. They were surrounding us, with their hands out." she said turning her hands, palms up.

Nick didn't know how to interpret this, so he asked, "What does it mean to you?"

"Well, I don't know if you want to hear this," she said, hesitantly. "But I think that if we find your treasure…I think we should use it to help these people," Cheyenne said, studying Nick's face for his response.

Nick had an incredulous look on his face, "You mean, risk my life and my friend's lives to find a treasure—and then…just *give* most of it away?"

"Something like that," Cheyenne said, smiling. She was able to find the humor in it when Nick said it out loud.

"Sounds like something only a crazy person would do." He paused then added, "…or me." His own words struck him funny and he started to laugh.

"Yeah, it does," she said, laughing with him. She was glad Nick was starting to agree with her idea.

Richard smiled and said, "Many times, what the Creator asks of us seems crazy. But that is only because we are unable to see his bigger plan."

"Maybe you're right," Nick nodded to Richard. He thought about the old man's words before he broke the silence and said, "Let me ask you about something."

The old Indian looked at Nick's face and he could tell that he was ready to learn more—he had waited long enough.

"All right," Richard agreed.

"If I'm going to do this," Nick started. "I need to make sense of all this. What happened with the Jesuits and those Indians up in the mountains?"

"I can only tell you the stories and legends I have heard," Richard said.

"I need to know." Nick said.

Richard nodded slowly, "Yes, you do."And so, Richard began to tell the stories of the Jesuits and the Indians—the stories that had been passed down to him many years before. Nick and Cheyenne listened intently as he spoke.

They both nodded their heads in understanding when he had finished. Nick was glad he had come to sit with Richard. Once again, he was amazed at the experiences he was having with both he and Cheyenne.

He also thought about what Cheyenne had said about the treasure. Nick knew that she might be right. He didn't know how the others would feel, or what they would want to do. More than likely, they would disagree with him. Maybe even think he had lost his mind. But he wasn't too worried about the gold anymore—his mind was on other things. After months and months, his gold fever had finally broken—it was like a huge burden being lifted from his shoulders.

They started on their long drive back to town. Cheyenne could see that Nick was quiet and deep in thought. Finally she turned and asked him, "Have you decided what you'll do?"

"There's someone else I need to talk to," Nick said resolutely. "Then I can make my decision."

"Okay," Cheyenne said, still curious but not wanting to press him too much.

But for now she wondered who was it that he wanted to talk with. And why it would have any bearing on his decision.

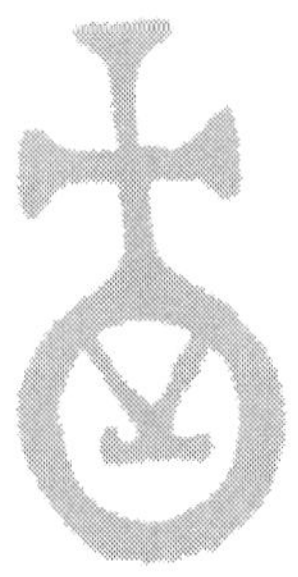

# Chapter 20

## Jesuit Markings

Nick drove his car down Central Avenue. He pulled into a restaurant parking lot, across the street from St. Francis Xavier Catholic Church. That's where he waited on this Sunday afternoon.

It was almost two thirty before he saw the man he was waiting for come out of the church. Nick got out of the car quickly, but it turned out, he didn't have to hurry. The man was crossing the street, on his way to the restaurant.

"Father Martin!" Nick called out.

The old priest turned around. "Yes?" he answered. A surprised look overcame his face when he realized that it was Nick calling to him.

Nick approached the old priest with his hand out, saying, "Father Martin, my name is Nick Rivera." The priest reluctantly took Nick's hand and gave it a lackluster shake. Nick continued, "I don't know if you remember, but I met you a while back in Agent Goldberg's office?"

"Why yes," he said, studying Nick's face. "You're the young man who was looking for treasure up in the mountains."

"Agent Diaz said you might be around here. I wonder if I could have a word with you?" The old priest looked resistant, but Nick was determined. "I'll buy your lunch," he said, smiling while pointing to the restaurant.

Father Martin looked at the restaurant and then back at Nick. "All right then, I suppose," he acquiesced.

They took a booth in the back of the restaurant. Father Martin ordered a sandwich, but Nick just ordered a cola. He wasn't really hungry. After they ordered, they made small talk until the food arrived. They found that they had something in common—Father Martin had spent time in Alaska as a young man.

"Where did you live?" Nick asked with interest.

"Oh, I worked on some of the fishing boats in Sitka and Juneau. But that was many years ago—I'm sure those towns have changed quite a bit."

"Yes, they have," Nick agreed. "I'm sure they're not as wild as when you were there."

"I couldn't tell you about that. I'm afraid I spent most of my time out on the boats," the old priest shared.

The waitress brought their order to the table before Nick changed the subject.

"So, Father Martin," he started. "You are somewhat of a church historian, right?"

"Yes," Father Martin smiled modestly. "Somewhat."

Nick continued, "Well, I've been doing some research about the Jesuits in this area—during the sixteenth and seventeenth century."

"Uh-huh,"

"The time of the priests like Father Kino..." Nick looked at the old priest for a reaction.

"Yes, I'm familiar with some of them," Father Martin acknowledged dryly. "They taught the Indians how to raise cattle. And how to grow different crops."

Nick pressed, "And they converted them to Christianity?"

"Yes, they built many missions and churches with vistas."

"What about mining?" Nick asked. "Were they overseeing any mining operations?"

"Oh no," Father Martin said dismissively. "The King of Spain did not allow it. It was illegal for them to operate any mines."

"No mining?" Nick asked again. He wanted to be sure of what the old priest was saying.

Father Martin waved his hand, "Those are all old legends," he insisted. "Fantastic stories about 'Jesuit gold mines' are far more interesting than the true mundane stories about farming."

Nick politely nodded, "Well, what can you tell me about the expulsion?" he asked. "It seems to be kind of mysterious."

"It was King Carlos III of Spain who made the decision," Father Martin explained. "You see, at the time, the Jesuits were strong supporters of the Spanish Inquisition. But the Enlightenment movement was spreading and that's what King Carlos supported. Portugal had already expelled all the Jesuits out of their territories earlier. So, he sent out letters to his representatives wherever there were Jesuit holdings. The letters gave no reason, nor made any formal charges. They simply said that after midnight on June 25th 1767, all Jesuits were to be arrested and marched to Vera Cruz port, where they were shipped back to Europe."

"So, they suddenly woke up one day," Nick postulated. "And found that they were enemies of Spain, and under arrest?"

"In simple terms, yes," Father Martin agreed. "There had been accusations of espionage, and treason before. But none of it was true."

"Interesting," Nick said, taking a sip of his cola.

"It was a dark time for the Order." the old priest offered.

Nick gave him time to eat more of his sandwich before he continued with his questions.

"What can you tell me about a Father Neve?"

"Father Neve?" Father Martin repeated. He had a puzzled look on his face like he was surprised to be asked about him.

"Yes. Are you familiar with him?" Nick questioned.

"Yes, I'm familiar," Father Martin said curtly. But he seemed very reluctant to discuss him further.

"Well," Nick pressed. "He was the last Jesuit priest assigned to this area. Do you know if he left any writings or if he had anything to say about what happened?"

Father Martin looked briefly around the restaurant wondering what he should tell Nick about this. Finally he said, "Yes, he left a journal," He rationalized that there would be no harm in telling Nick this much. Maybe this would even give him the opportunity to discourage Nick from searching for the treasure. "Father Neve had only been in the area a few years before the expulsion. And he was younger than most of the other priests. You see, becoming a priest became less appealing to many of the younger people of the time. Most of the priests in the Jesuit Order were older men. So, being younger than most, he was able to survive the long march back down to Mexico, as well as the ordeal of being shipped back to Europe. Many of his brother-priests were not so fortunate."

"Did he say why he thought they were expelled?"

"No, he didn't say. Like others, he had heard of the false accusations about plotting against the King."

"But it wasn't true?" Nick asked.

"No, it wasn't true," Father Martin repeated with certitude.

The two of them then sat in silence. Nick waited until he was finished eating before he spoke again.

"Well Father, thank you for your time." Nick said, wanting to put him at ease. "You're very knowledgeable."

"You're welcome," the priest said. "I sincerely hope you aren't planning to go out there in the desert again."

Nick was cautious about revealing too much. "I'm still thinking about it," he said.

"Please!" Father Martin pleaded, somewhat exasperated. "You can save yourself a lot of time and energy—go back to Alaska and forget about this whole thing."

"I suppose you're right." he said with a bit of resignation.

"You'll be better off," the priest encouraged.

The waitress brought over the check to their table and both men smiled at her. When she left, Nick took the opportunity to press him one more time. "There's something that I was wondering about."

"Yes? What's that?"

"Well," Nick started. "You said earlier that the Jesuit priest were not doing any mining."

"That's correct!" The priest said with conviction.

"But, if that's the case," Nick questioned. "Why did the King and his soldiers have to carry out the orders for expulsion in such secrecy?"

Father Martin looked a bit puzzled, trying to understand the implications of Nick's question. "What do you mean?" he asked.

Nick held the fingers of his right hand to his forehead. "I mean, unless they were trying to catch them in the middle of doing something they weren't supposed to be doing…"

Father Martin cleared his throat, he appeared to have been caught off guard by the question. "Well," he said, searching for possibilities. "I suppose they didn't want them to escape."

Gesturing with his palm up, Nick quickly asked, "Where could they escape to?"

Now a bit rattled, the old priest said, "I…I don't know, I'm afraid I couldn't tell you what their reasoning was."

"I understand." Nick said coolly. "I just have one more question Father—"

"Look," Father Martin interrupted. "There's no treasure of gold out there," He was now getting visibly irritated with Nick's line of questioning.

"Well, what about the gold and silver bars that have been found with the Jesuit markings on them?"

The priest shook his head negatively as he thought of what to say. "Look, there are many things that show up in the antiquities market—people trying to make money—but this doesn't mean that they're authentic."

Nick, once again, pretended the priest was convincing. "Maybe you're right."

"Take my advice," he pushed. "And go back to Alaska. I'm sure you can make more money fishing up there, than you can looking for fictitious gold down here."

"Thanks for the advice," Nick said politely, nodding his head, as he picked up the check. "Again Father, thank you for your time." With that, Nick stood up, left a tip on the table and went to the counter to pay.

After paying the check, he walked outside. The contrast between the air-conditioned restaurant and blasting heat of outdoors was startling.  He felt the hot sun beating down on his face as he got into his car. With the windows up, it was a good 30 degrees hotter than it was outside. He forgot to leave a crack in the windows before going to lunch to let the heat escape. Everything he touched was blisteringly hot. So, he rolled down the windows and started the engine running the air conditioner on full blast. Once the inside started cooling down, he rolled the windows back up and turned down the air-conditioner. Only then did he pull out his cellphone and call Cheyenne.

"Hey!" She said, excitedly. "What's going on?"

"I just had a talk with someone."

"And how did it go?" She asked.

"It was very interesting," he said cryptically.

"Yeah? What did he say?"

Nick paused for a second. "He said I should forget about any gold and go back to Alaska."

"Okay," she said, dejected. "So, what do you wanna do?"

"I wanna go find some gold!"

# Chapter 21

## The Trap

It was the afternoon of July 29th when the monsoon rains poured down over the desert. Since they couldn't ride, the team was in the office. Some cleaning their gear, Cheyenne and Darren were playing video games—they were trying to kill time and fight the boredom that was setting in.

"I'm getting tired of this waiting around," Speed said to no one in particular, as he sheathed the knife he had been sharpening.

"Well," Darren said, as he set down his game controller and looked out the window. "I don't think we're gonna be doing anything now."

"Wrong!" Nick's voice boomed as he entered the office. He had been watching the skies too. The rain may have been dampening their spirits, but it was just what Nick had been waiting for. "It's time to get ready!" He announced.

Cheyenne was startled, "Get ready?" she asked.

Nick looked around the room at his team with a steely gaze. He could see the anticipation on their faces. Finally, his face lightened, and with a smile he cheered, "Let's go on a treasure hunt!"

"Yeehaaa!" Speed yelled with excitement. These were exactly the words that he and his team had been waiting to hear.

The next morning, he and the others packed their gear. That afternoon they hauled their four-wheelers to the staging area at the edge of the Superstition Mountains.

Speed and Jim drove the large truck back into the small canyon, as far as it would go. Nick and Sammy drove the others out there in Sammy's SUV. Sammy would stay in the camp, waiting for them.

Unloading the four-wheelers, they made their camp in the secluded canyon. It was there that they made their final preparations. They topped off their vehicles with fuel, checked their weapons, ropes, climbing gear, lights, etc. From here they could get an early start in the morning. With any luck, they could make it to the Mountain by the end of the day.

Nick had a schedule he wanted to keep. With the heavy rains coming late, it would already be August 1st before they would be able to work the site. But with the Army taking over the land, and turning the remote area into a firing range, it could become even more dangerous.

That night they sat around the campfire, after all their checks and double checks had been made. They contemplated their endeavor. Not sure what the next day would bring.

"So, gentlemen, tomorrow we start our big adventure." Cheyenne said.

"Yes we will." Speed agreed.

"You know," Jim said, looking at Cheyenne. "Something's been bothering me. All of us here are adventurers in our own way, or looking to make a buck. But you, you're a helper. I just don't figure you for this."

"Maybe I just figured a bigger way to help people," she said.

"How's that?" Jim asked.

"Money from that treasure can help a lot of people." Cheyenne said, drawing strange looks from all the others—all except Nick.

"That money's gonna help me very nicely." Sammy said.

"I tell you what. That money's gonna help me to tell my boss to go shove it." Speed chuckled.

"Even people with money can have problems." she said.

"Well, those problems are a lot easier to deal with if you have money." Sammy said.

"We got a big day tomorrow guys. I think we all need to turn in," Nick said. He wanted them well rested. And besides, there was no use in arguing about money they didn't have.

They all agreed, and soon they were all laying in their sleeping bags, trying to sleep. The excitement and possibilities of what they were doing kept them all tossing and turning—all of them except Nick. He slept soundly and worry-free. He was sleeping better lately—better that he had in a long time. He was at ease—like he was where he should be, doing what he should be doing.

"Wake up! Wake up!" Nick yelled, as the sun was starting to come up. "You're burning daylight."

"What?" Someone asked? Others were moaning.

"Burning daylight?" Jim grumbled. "I don't see any daylight."

Nick looked to the eastern horizon where the sky was barely becoming a pale gradient of light. "You will shortly." He said, nodding towards the east.

Nick sat quietly, away from the others. He watched the sunlight break over the mountains. It was a beautiful, peaceful sight. As he watched, he contemplated the day ahead of him and prayed for the safety of his friends. When he finished, he returned to the camp for breakfast.

It wasn't long before everyone was up and moving around. Sammy was being unusually helpful. He scrambled some eggs and cooked some sausage on a Coleman gas stove that they brought. They all ate heartily—it fueled them up for their long day.

After their breakfast, they loaded their four-wheelers and started down the trail. Nick led the way, since he knew where to go. He was followed by Darren, and then Cheyenne. Jim and then Speed brought up the rear. Speed was riding the larger 4-wheeler, and pulling a heavy duty trailer.

They made their way along the rocky trail. It was slow, but steady going on the four-wheelers. Still, they were making good time. At this rate they would make the petroglyphs by late afternoon.

They made a long stop at midday. They drank Gatorade and ate energy bars. The heat was sweltering. It was at least 110 degrees, maybe hotter. The desert heat was dry, so the moisture evaporated off your skin before you had a chance to sweat. Water took up most of the space of supplies on their machines. It was also the heaviest. But without enough of it, they wouldn't survive the expedition much less work a mine.

Nick rode along until he came to the area of the petroglyphs. The area to his right opened up, then the higher area dropped sharply. That was where the petroglyphs were. Ahead, after the trail opened up, it narrowed down again. Nick slowed down, looking for any signs of company.

When he came to the open area, he stopped on a flat space, before the hill made a sharp incline, leading to the petroglyphs. That was when Nick saw movement on the ridgeline. It was them.

Nick sounded his air horn to warn the others. He turned to see where everyone was. Jim and Speed were far enough back—they made a quick retreat. Cheyenne and Darren were not far behind him. So, he waved for them to get away. Cheyenne headed up the trail as fast as she could, with Darren trying to keep up.

Nick looked up the hill. There was one person up by the petroglyphs to the right, and another one closer to him, almost straight ahead. Behind him, was a trail going over a smaller hill. Nick thought it was his best chance.

He gunned his four-wheeler and headed straight for the man. The man pointed his gun, but then realized that the ATV would still run him over. So, in a panic, he lowered his arm and dove out of the way. Nick drove right past him, up the trail to the top of the hill. He heard a gunshot from behind, but it seemed to go over his head.

Nick stopped at the top of the hill, long enough to see a vehicle coming down one side of another hill to block Cheyenne and Darren's escape. The vehicle didn't look like it would be able to block Cheyenne's escape, but it could stop Darrin's.

'Dammit!', Nick thought. He couldn't let anything happen to Darren. He promised his sister he would keep him safe. Decidedly, he turned the four-wheeler around and headed back down the hill. He raised his hands as he got closer to the two men—the one from the petroglyphs and the other was the one he almost ran over.

They kept their guns on him as he came down the hill. They removed his short-handled pump shotgun from his four-wheeler when he stopped. He could see that the other men had caught Darren—and now they were bringing him up the trail, to them.

"I'm sorry Uncle Nick," Darren said apologetically when he got close.

One of the men was driving his four-wheeler as Darren walked ahead of it. The other vehicle came behind.

Nick stared at Darren with concern, "It's okay. You tried."

They were all standing together when Nick noticed another four-wheeler heading towards them. They all turned to look. It was Cheyenne. She should have kept going to get away. Why was she coming back?

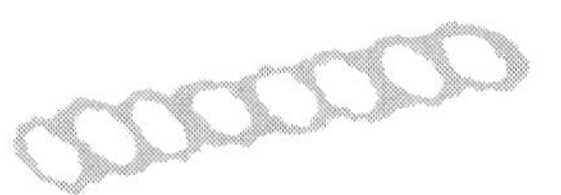

# Chapter 22

## Captured

Alameda's men sat the three down together on the hillside. The men contacted their boss on a hand held radio, telling him they had found the 'big man' he was looking for. Now they waited for their boss to arrive.

"What happened to your friends?" Cheyenne asked Nick, incredulously. The distain and sarcasm in her voice was obvious.

"I think they got away." Nick replied under his breath as he looked around at his captors.

"Ran away, is more like it," Cheyenne said disgustedly. "All their brave, macho, crap, and then they chicken-out." She rolled her eyes and looked away.

"You should have kept going." Nick said trying to keep his voice low.

"Go where?" she whispered forcefully. "Besides," she continued, as she looked at Diego's men with contempt. "I'm not afraid. We have to find a way to turn the tables on these guys."

"Now listen," Nick whispered with command. "I don't want you trying anything until I tell you to—understand?"

Cheyenne looked at him questioningly, but nodded in the belief that Nick must have some plan.

"Hey!" Nick called out to his captors, as he stood up. "I need to take a piss!"

The apparent leader motioned for him to go, and then assigned another to go with him. Nick walked up the hill, heading toward the petroglyphs. Using this ruse was the only distraction Nick could think of. If his luck held out, it might even work.

"That's far enough," the man said, wanting to stop the climb up the hill.

"Please, just a little farther," Nick said, looking and nodding toward Cheyenne.

The man looked down the hill at the group—they were still fairly visible to the woman. "All right," he said.

Nick made it up to the petroglyphs. He looked down at the writings on the rocks. He saw the section that he believed lead to the location of the treasure. He then found the section that wasn't visible—the part that should be pinpointing the location. Nick was about to see if George Rogers' idea would work.

Nick urinated on that section. As the moisture from his urine hit the rock, Nick couldn't believe his eyes, the ancient markings soon became visible. He memorized the symbols. It would be his only chance to see them.

"All right Señor," his guard said. "Let's go."

"Just a minute," Nick said, zipping up his pants. The sun's heat was quickly evaporating the moisture from the rocks. In a moment, the markings were gone. Satisfied, Nick turned and walked back down the hill with his escort. When they returned to the group, he sat down with Cheyenne and Darren.

It wasn't long before they saw a plume of dust of a white SUV coming down the trail. He knew it was Diego Alameda by the way his men reacted.

"Well!" Diego said, getting out of the passenger's side door. Nick recognized the driver as one of the men he had fought with in his first unwelcome meeting out here.

"Good to see you again, Mr. Montana. Or is it Mr. Rivera? Or perhaps you're using a different name today?"

"Rivera will do," Nick said, as he stood up.

"And your friends?" He said, motioning to Cheyenne and Darren, who were still sitting.

"This is Cheyenne," Nick said, pointing first to her, then to Darren. "And this is Darren."

"My pleasure," he said, nodding to them both. "I am Diego." He held his arms out and turned around toward his men and then back to Nick, Cheyenne and Darren. "You see… we can all be civilized here."

"Sure." Nick said, eager to keep everyone calm.

"My men tell me that you had two other friends that escaped."

"I think maybe they just decided to leave."

"Uh-huh. But you… you have come back for the treasure?" Diego asked in an interrogating tone. "Is that it?"

"I don't know anything about a treasure. We just came out here to go camping."

"Well then," Diego said, nodding to his men. "If that's true, then you are of no value to me."

Diego's men cocked their weapons and lowered them at Cheyenne and Darren.

"Wait, wait!" Nick shouted. "Okay, maybe I do know something."

"Uh-huh," Diego said. "I thought that might help your memory. Now, tell me how to find this treasure."

"Well, I'm not sure," Nick said, turning briefly to Darren and Cheyenne with a slight shrug. "But I think I can show you—on one condition." He said turning back to Diego.

"What's that?"

"I get you the treasure, and you let us go—with half of the treasure."

Diego laughed. "You're not really in a position to negotiate here," he said, shaking his head. Then gesturing his hand toward Darren, "I could just kill you all now."

Nick glanced back at Cheyenne and Darren and back to Diego. "Yes, you could." He agreed reluctantly. "But if I *do* know how to find the treasure, it would die with me."

Diego took his time, thinking it over. This Rivera was a clever man—he didn't trust him. However, maybe he really had found a way to get the treasure. Besides, he could always kill them afterwards.

"Come on," Nick implored, "you know I wouldn't have come back if I didn't know something."

Diego looked around at his men and back at Nick. "All right," he said. "I will share the treasure with you—at seventy-thirty."

"What?"

"I'm afraid that is the best deal you will get today my friend," Diego said threateningly. He did not want his men to see him out negotiated by people who were virtual prisoners.

"Okay," Nick relented.

"So, how do we proceed?"

"We keep moving. I think we can make the Mountain before sundown."

"The Mountain?"

"Yes, there's a certain mountain we're looking for. If I'm right, I'll find the signs."

"Okay then," Diego agreed, looking at the sun. There was still plenty of daylight left. "Show us the way, amigo."

Diego's men checked the four-wheelers for weapons. Nick was the only one who had anything—his shotgun and K-bar knife. They put Darren in the SUV under guard, and let Nick and Cheyenne drive their four-wheelers. One of the men rode behind them on Darren's.

Nick led the way. He drove his machine hard for two reasons. One, he wanted to make sure they got to the mountain before dark. They were still pressed for time. And two, he wanted to see if the SUVs could keep up. They couldn't. It was harder for them to maneuver around the large rocks on the trail.

The sun was starting to go down when they finally made it to the mountain. There was a relatively flat area in the narrow canyon, in between two mountains. That's where Nick told them they needed to make camp.

When Nick and Cheyenne got off their machines, they immediately started refueling them. The others were still making their way to the camp.

"Why did you make a deal with him?" Cheyenne said quietly. "He's not gonna keep his word."

"Of course he's not," Nick whispered forcefully.

Cheyenne was confused over Nick's strategy. "Then why did you do that?" she questioned him.

"I'm just buying time." Nick responded, looking back over his shoulder at the approaching SUVs.

"We have to get their guns somehow." Cheyenne suggested.

"No! We have to get inside that mountain," Nick whispered, adamantly.

"How?" She asked, still confused over his motives.

“If everything goes right, I’ll show you tomorrow morning.”

“If everything goes right? What does *that* mean?” She demanded.

“Just try to trust me.” Nick whispered as he nodded toward the approaching vehicles.

They topped off their four-wheelers just as the SUVs were pulling up. Diego got out and looked around.

“Okay, where is it?”

“Tomorrow.” Nick said with confidence.

“Tomorrow?” Diego said, obviously angry.

“Yeah, it’s too late to see anything now,” Nick explained. It was already dusk. “We should be able to see the signs tomorrow.”

# Chapter 23

## Heart of the Cross

Diego's men gathered firewood to build a fire. It took them a while, as wood was scarce out there. They were lucky enough to find an old dead ironwood tree that they could cut up for it. They all set up their sleeping bags around the campfire. For a land that could be so hot during the day, it could be unusually cool at night.

Diego had eight men, including himself. Nick needed to track them all as best as he could. If they were to have a hope to escape, he would need to have an idea of where everyone was.

Nick, Cheyenne and Darren set their bags down together, across the campfire from Diego and his men. They had already taken Nick's weapons. The two groups sat on their sleeping bags, looking across the fire at each other.

"Señor Rivera, I will not have you all tied up." Diego said. "But I want your word that you will not try anything tonight."

"No problem," Nick said, shaking his head. "Nowhere to go out here at night anyway."

"Good, I'll take you at your word."

"And I'll take you at *your* word, Diego." Nick said.

"Of course," Diego said with a smile. "We must trust one another, no?"

"Yes, I agree."

"Good," Diego said. "So, let me ask you something. Why would a treasure hunter like yourself, come here to look for this treasure?"

"What do you mean?" Nick said.

"That's what treasure hunters do." Cheyenne added.

"Yes, but if you really found a big treasure in Florida." Diego said. "You wouldn't have to come out here to look for this one."

"Very insightful." Nick said. "And you're right. Maybe I didn't really find a big treasure. I was just one of several investors with a big overhead to pay off. Maybe you could explain that to some of my friends."

"I understand." Diego nodded.

"And since we're being honest with each other," Nick said. "You don't strike me as someone who's desperate for money. What's driving you Diego?"

Suddenly, all eyes shifted to him. Even his own men seemed to want to know his real motivation. Realizing this, Diego decided to tell them the real story.

"Okay Señor," Diego said, looking around. "Since we're both treasure hunters, I might as well tell you. You see, many, many years ago, my great grandfather worked for the Peraltas. They were a wealthy family in these parts.

They had a large number of men, and set up a big gold mining operation here in the mountains. That was, until they were discovered by the Apaches. They didn't want anyone on their lands. So, they waited, gathering more and more men every day. Peralta and his men knew the Indians were watching and waiting. They dug as much gold as they could. But when they thought it was getting too dangerous, they made a run for it."

"And what happened?" Cheyenne asked. She wanted to know as much about this as she could.

"They waited too long," Diego said, nodding his head. "The Apaches followed them. Waited until they were in the perfect spot, and then they ambushed them—the site's not too far from here. They call it, 'Peralta's Massacre'."

"They killed everyone?" Cheyenne asked woefully.

"Almost everyone." Diego said. "There were two survivors. They escaped, and made their way down to Sonora Mexico."

"Did they ever come back?" Cheyenne asked.

"Well, when they got to Sonora," he continued, "they told their story to a couple of old miners—Jacob Waltz and his partner. It wasn't long before the three of them rode back up here to find the gold."

"Wait, you said the *three* of them?" Cheyenne asked.

"Yes, you see, my great grandfather had no desire to return," he said sadly. "One brush with death was enough for him. He was afraid."

"So, you're here to get his share?" Nick asked.

"Something like that. But you see, I am not afraid." Diego said, looking around at his men. They were all listening intently.

"Well, you wouldn't be the first." Nick said.

"What do you mean?" Diego asked.

"I mean lots of people have gotten scared off from this place. They say it's cursed by the Indians." Nick said, looking around. "People see things, floating skulls… nightmares."

Nick looked around at the faces of Diego's men. It was having an effect. They were starting to look nervous.

"Eh! Superstitions!" Diego said, trying to reassure them. "Old wive's tales used to scare children. Surely you don't believe them, do you?"

"Of course I do. But then, I'm part Indian. They say the treasure will never be given up to just anyone—only those with a pure heart. Why do you think no one has ever been able to find it in all these years?"

"Maybe he's right, jefe?" One of his men said. They all seemed worried now. It was just what Nick wanted. He wanted them to question their motives. It might make them more inclined to quit. Especially if they worried about Diego sharing any treasure with them.

"Nonsense!" Diego grumbled.

"You know," Nick said, wanting to keep their attention. "The Jesuits were here long before the Peraltas. They say they got the Indians to work the mines for them."

"Yes?" Diego said, curious.

"That's what they say." Nick answered. "They also say that they buried a lot of them alive when they left."

"You mean buried alive, in the mine?" One of Diego's younger men asked. He didn't look to be much older than Darren.

"Yes, buried in the mine. They say that's why their spirits roam around out here," Nick said, waving his hand around. "According to old Indian legends, there was a young couple who helped the Jesuits. They spoke the language and helped convert many of the Indians to Christianity. Now, when the last priest left, they sent most of the Indians away. But the ones who had knowledge of the mine, they gathered them up. They placed them inside the mine, and then they sealed the entrance."

"In that mountain?" One of his men asked, noticeably worried.

"Yes!" Nick said, in a loud whisper. Diego's men were listening intently now, so he continued. "And the Indian couple, after being betrayed, they vowed vengeance—even in the afterlife. They say their spirits won't rest until they have their revenge. And that their spirits roam these mountains, cursing all those who seek to find the gold."

"Enough of this!" Diego barked. He knew from their faces that these stories were shaking his men's confidence. "Time for sleep! Tomorrow we will find this treasure, spirits or no spirits."

Nick got an almost imperceptable grin on his face.

Diego set his men up a rotation to stand guard as everyone prepared to go to sleep. Nick settled on his sleeping bag, confident that he had done as much as he could to rattle Diego's men. He just hoped they would have enough time the following day to do what they needed to do.

"Nice stories," Cheyenne said quietly, after she settled in her sleeping bag, laying to Nick's left.

"Think I scared 'em?" Nick asked with a smile.

"Scared the hell out of me." Darren whispered, on Nick's right.

Darren noticed the smile on Nick's face.

"Well, by the sound of his snores, Diego is already asleep. I wonder what he's dreaming about?" Darren whispered. He looked over at Nick who gave him a wink, like he knew something. But he offered no more, so Darren closed his eyes and fell asleep too.

Nick woke up as daylight was breaking. Everyone else was still asleep. Except for one of Diego's men who was standing guard, and he seemed half asleep. But, it didn't matter. Nick wasn't going to try to run. And if he made a move for their guns, there could be shooting. Who knows who might get shot? So, he got the fire going again and heated up some water. Right now, he just wanted some coffee. When it was hot enough, he mixed in his instant grounds.

It was when he took his first sip, that he realized something. Two of the sleeping bags were empty. He looked around but didn't see the former occupants anywhere.

When Diego woke up, he hollered in Spanish to the others and woke them all up. It wasn't long before he realized that two of his men had run off in the night. They must have slipped away on foot. He would have heard any engine start up, and the vehicle and four-wheelers were still there. He had scheduled his men to stand guard in two-hour shifts. That meant that someone standing guard must have dozed off. Diego gave his guard, Jorge, a kick and cussed at him for falling asleep.

"It wasn't me, patrón! I didn't fall asleep," Jorge protested.

Diego waved his hands dismissively and cursed the two who left for being cowards. He then threatened to shoot anyone else who tried to leave.

Nick pulled out some instant oatmeal and insisted Cheyenne and Darren eat it. It could be a long physical day—and they couldn't be sure when they would eat again. Diego's men were ill prepared for this trek into the desert. So, besides sharing their coffee, they also gave them some energy bars. The men seemed grateful—the way Nick saw it, they could be civil. Diego's men hadn't hurt anyone—yet.

"Gracias Señorita," Jorge said to Cheyenne. He seemed to be particularly enamored with her.

She politely smiled and said, "You're welcome."

They all drank a full pot of coffee and then had to heat up another. Diego's men quickly gobbled up the energy bars.

"It's morning, amigo," Diego said. "So, when will we see it?"

Nick sat quietly sipping his second cup of coffee, then casually said, "We have plenty of time," He took a bite of an energy bar and pointed to the eastern horizon, "The sun has to come up over the mountains first." He said while still chewing.

Diego looked intently to the east and then nodded his head in understanding to Nick. A few minutes later, he gave some instructions in Spanish to a couple of his men. Afterwards, they walked over to Nick and Cheyenne's four-wheelers and climbed on.

Nick stood up and shouted, "Hey, where are they going?"

The two ATVs revved up as Diego shouted over the roaring engines, "They are going to look for your two compadres. They could still be out there. We wouldn't want anything bad to happen to them, no? The desert is a dangerous place, amigo."

Nick looked over at the two vehicles—they still had supplies on them. "Okay, but have them leave the gear here," he said, commandingly. "We're gonna need it to get into the mountain."

Diego motioned to the two men to turn off the engines. "All right," he agreed. He then barked orders to his men in Spanish to remove the gear before they went on their search for Nick's other men. They removed all of it and then started the engines again—kicking up dust as they tore off into the desert.

With those two leaving, and the two last night, Diego was now down to three men. Nick knew he needed every edge he could get.

"Okay, it's sunrise. Now what?" Diego asked, anxiously.

Nick slowly scanned across the western horizon. The sun was starting to come up and it's golden light was just beginning to fall on the surrounding rocks. Then scanning to the east, he saw an unusual formation of rocks on the opposite side of the mountain.

"There!" He said pointing to the group of rocks about 300 yards away. "That's where we go."

Nick wasted no time—he immediately took off toward the small cluster of boulders and everyone quickly followed him. He helped Cheyenne and Diego up on top of the rocky outcropping. They stood there quietly for a time, as the sun rose behind them. They watched as Nick intently scanned the mountains.

"Over there!" He said confidently, pointing directly across from them.

Following his finger, they could hardly believe their eyes. The mountain seemed to transform in front of them. As the golden light washed over it, large, dark lines seemed to appear. The lines made the shape of a cross. However, at the top of the cross it curved into a hook, like a staff. They all looked on in amazement.

"What in the hell?" Diego said in disbelief. "I've never seen this out here before."

George Rogers had been right. He told Nick he thought there was a variation in the soil. And after the hard rain, the variations were more obvious now.

"Maybe it doesn't show itself to everyone," Nick said, smiling. He wasn't going to let them in on George's theory.

Diego dismissed Nick's taunt but was clearly impressed by the sign. "All right," He said. "How do you plan to get into it?"

Nick continued studying the mountain before turning to Cheyenne. "You think we can repel down from the top to where it intersects?" He pointed to the crossing lines on the staff and looked to her for her opinion.

"You mean, climb up from the side and tie off—repelling down the face over the cross?" She said, diagraming it with her hand.

Nick squinted at the cross, "Yeah."

"That's why you brought me." She said confidently.

"Diego!" Nick called. "I need you to place a man here to guide us to our spot."

Diego was opposed to the idea. "One of my men?" He questioned. "Maybe we should use your boy," Diego said, pointing to Darren.

Nick shrugged, "That'll work."

Diego seemed suspicious of Nick's willingness. "No," he said, after thinking about it. He realized it would be better to keep them all together on the mountain. "We can use my man."

"Okay," Nick said with an easy casualness. He then showed Diego's man Jorge, where they were going. They were going right to the heart of the cross. But, they would be too close to the markings to see where to go. So, they needed someone standing far back on these rocks to guide them.

They then hurried back to the camp. Nick, Cheyenne and Darren started getting their gear together. They put on their backpacks and grabbed their ropes.

"Before you go too far," Diego interrupted, pointing a gun at them. "Tell me what you intend to do."

Nick didn't like having a gun pointed at him. He raised his hands and gestured for Diego to put the gun down. He needed him to believe that they were going to cooperate. "Well," he said calmly. "We repel down the mountain to the heart of that cross. If I'm right, that's where the entrance into the mountain is. But, we'll have to dig it open with shovels and picks."

Diego recklessly waved the gun around like it was a pointing stick. "And what about us?" he asked.

"Well, you and your men stay at the top. When we get in, Cheyenne will come back and get you." Nick said nodding toward Cheyenne.

Diego was uncertain of Nick's plan. He needed to make sure that they didn't get out of his sight. "And what if you just keep going down the mountain?" He posed, threateningly.

Nick looked at Diego's three men. "Okay, then keep one of your men at the bottom of the mountain." He offered.

Diego kept searching his mind for possible problems with Nick's plan but couldn't find any. Finally he said, "All right."

Cheyenne gave Nick a funny look. It seemed to her like he was  helping them out. However, Nick was still focused on how to separate Diego's men as much as possible.

Diego placed a man at the bottom, as the rest of them walked south, to start the climb up the mountain. This would leave just Diego and his man, Juan, to watch them. However, Diego and his men still had the advantage—they had the guns.

When they arrived at a point just above the middle of the cross, Diego's man on the rock cluster hollered on the walkie-talkie for them to stop. With Cheyenne leading the way, they had made the climb in roughly forty-five minutes. Nick looked at his watch—it was almost nine o'clock. He wasn't sure how much time they had, but he didn't want to waste any.

When they got to the top, they set down their gear. Cheyenne began making repelling harnesses for herself, Nick and Darren, with carabiners and short ropes. She then tied off the ropes to some large boulders, throwing the free ends off the side of the mountain.

Diego and Juan stood there watching as Cheyenne hooked up herself, Nick and Darren to the long ropes. Nick had done some repelling in the Marine Corps, so he was familiar with what they needed to do. She repeated some quick instructions, how to keep the rope taut as you start your walk down the side of the mountain, how to hold the ropes away to drop down, and how to pull the rope tight behind them to stop. After a few minutes of this, they all started carefully down the mountainside.

Diego continued watching as the three slowly disappeared over the mountain's edge.

# Chapter 24

## Soul Mates

When they lowered themselves down to the intersection of the cross, Jorge called to Diego on the walkie-talkie and Diego hollered for them to stop. Luckily there seemed to be a small ledge at the same spot where they could stand, as well as an indentation with what looked like an old opening that was covered with rocks, all solidly wedged together with smaller debris and caliche mud.

The ledge was large enough for them to hold their footing while digging with tools. They began to dig into the rocks. Looking around, Nick thought he saw remnants of rope coming out of the rocks. Someone must have built a rope ladder or bridge, he thought. That would certainly make it much easier for anyone to get in and out of this place.

Nick swung a pickaxe as Cheyenne dug with a shovel. They tried to be careful, so as not to hit one another. The rocks and dirt seemed to be coming out easy on this section. It gave them confidence that they were in the right spot. Darren traded off with Cheyenne, giving her a needed rest.

Nick heard a big boom, coming from a distance behind him. He turned around to see dark clouds in the east. It was thunder from the monsoon rainclouds headed towards them. It looked like a big storm, but he wasn't sure how far away it was.

Darren spun around on his rope and asked nervously, "What's that?"Nick grabbed him by the shoulder and pulled him back around. He patted Darren on the back and in a reassuring tone said, "Monsoon rains—headed this way—keep digging."

After a while, they stopped and took a water break. The digging was hard work and now the sun was beating down on them—adding heat to the dusty work. Nick thought the monsoons would be a nice relief from the heat.

Rocks, small boulders, and debris were tumbling down the rock face as they cleared just enough space in the opening to fit their bodies comfortably. When they had cleared enough of the entrance, Nick and Darren unhooked their harnesses from the rope. They no longer needed them for stability.

Diego noticed that the ropes went slack. "Did you open the entrance?" Diego hollered down.

"Almost!" Nick yelled in return.

"Send the girl back up!" Diego yelled.

Nick sighed in exasperation, then yelling, "Just a minute!"

"No, Señor! Send her now!" Diego demanded.

Nick turned to Cheyenne and quietly said, "You better go back up."

"You sure?" She whispered.

"Yeah, it'll be okay," he said, reassuring her.

Nick and Darren kept digging as she went back to the top. It wasn't long before they broke through and hit open air. The air was much cooler, but the smell was awful—it was a sickeningly pungent musty odor. But they had to go on. They kept digging until Nick could turn sideways and make his way into the cave.

"Oh God," Darren said. "What's that smell?"

"If I had to guess," Nick said. "I'd say it was very old dead bodies."

"I was afraid of that." Darren said under his breath.

They turned on their battery-powered headlamps so that they could see into the blinding darkness of the cave. With Darren right behind him, Nick held along the sides of the tunnel and made his way slowly. Within just a few steps, he came upon the first skeleton—then another, and another.

The narrow passageway began widening until the light from their headlamps revealed it opening to a large chamber. As he entered the chamber, the real horror hit him. There were several dozen skeletons covering the floor. From the sparse remainders of their clothing, they appeared to be Indians. If that was true, then the stories were right. They were buried in here alive. It appeared that some had tried to dig their way out, by hand, without success.

Nick looked around the cave. It went back quite a way and there was a smaller chamber to the side with a large boulder in the middle of it. On the far wall of the main room, was a large cross about two feet high. Nick brushed off the dark colored surface—it appeared to be covered with a layer of dirt. As he began wiping the dirt away, he suddenly saw that familiar glint of yellow. The cross appeared to be made of solid gold.

It was placed above a large flat stone that looked like some sort of altar. This must have been a ceremonial area, Nick thought. As he continued looking around, his eyes were drawn to two skeletons in the corner. Their bones seemed intertwined, like they had died in each other's arms. It gave Nick a sick feeling, thinking of what these people must have felt. For a moment, he was lost in thoughts of empathy.

"What the hell is this?" Darren said, almost in shock.

"They were buried alive." Nick said, starting to refocus. He pulled off his backpack and emptied its contents behind a rock. "Find a place to hide your stuff."

Darren looked at him confused, "Why?"

"Just do it!" Nick insisted. He then pulled out his camera and started taking pictures of the skeletons. There wasn't much light from their headlamps, so he used the flash on the camera.

After taking pictures, he looked again at the two skeletons that were huddled together. It wasn't hard to imagine their strong love for one another. He felt a strange connection to them. And now, for some reason, he began to think of the Indian girl he had seen in his vision in the sweat lodge. Was it connected, he wondered? What did it all mean? And suddenly, as he looked at the two skeletons, the idea of soulmates came to him—the idea of loving someone through life and death. While he was thinking about it all, he heard a voice coming from the entrance.

"God this smells awful," he heard Cheyenne say. Soon she was in the cave with Diego and Juan following.

"What did you find?" Diego hollered.

"Oh my God!" Cheyenne gasped in a hushed voice, looking around at all the skeletons.

"Found a lot of bones—and this," Nick said, putting the camera in his pocket. He pointed to the golden cross on the wall.

Not seeing anything else of value, Diego quickly pulled out a large knife and began to dig the cross out of the wall.

Cheyenne was still in shock from all the skeletal remains. "So, it's true," she said with sadness. "They killed all of these people."

"Yes, it's true." Nick said with empathy.

Diego had no concern about the dead. He wasn't about to leave empty handed. If the cross was solid gold, it would have quite a value. After digging it out, he placed it in a canvas bag and then pulled out his pistol.

"Over there, my friends." Diego said, motioning them to the far wall with his gun—away from the entrance. He hadn't been sure what to do with them, but last night he had a powerful dream. An old Indian spoke to him, and told him what to do.

Nick raised his hands and reminded him, "We had a deal, remember?"

"Yes, but you see, your spirit friends came to me last night." Diego said, moving towards the entrance with Juan. "I don't think they like you too much. They said I should leave you in here with them."

Well, at least he wasn't going to shoot them, Nick thought. Diego wasn't the kind to murder numerous people face to face. Easier to bury them and not think about their actual death.

"Your lights." Diego said, motioning to their headlamps.

"Not the lights!" Darren protested.

"I'm afraid you're going to have to get used to the dark." Diego said, pulling out a small stick of dynamite out of his pocket. He took their lights and moved with Juan, out to the entrance.

"How ironic." Cheyenne said.

"What's that?" Nick asked.

"That we meet the same fate as these people," she said. Looking around she was also drawn to the apparent skeletal couple, huddled together. It gave her chills seeing them.

There was some light coming into the cave from the entrance. Nick began searching for his things.

"Cover your ears," Nick said to Cheyenne and Darren.

"Why," Darren asked.

"Just do it!" Nick shouted. "And get down!"

They crouched down, covering their ears just as they heard a large blast come from the entrance. And then, everything went completely dark.

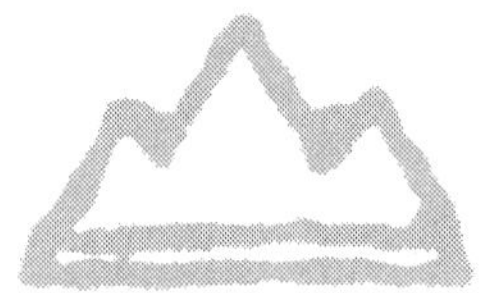

# Chapter 25

## Mountain of Gold

Gravel and dust filled the large chamber from the blast—and the three were coughing—shaken but thankfully still alive. Nick fumbled around in the dark—searching for the gear that he stashed away to hide it from Diego.

"Who grabbed my ass?" Cheyenne yelled in the darkness.

"Wasn't me." Darren chuckled.

"Well, somebody did!" She protested

"Well, I didn't do it." Darren said defensively, and then he quickly realized the direness of their situation. "Are we gonna die Uncle Nick?"

"Yes." Nick said calmly.

"I knew it!" Darren panicked.

"Someday… but I don't think it'll be today," Nick added coolly. He cracked and shook a glow-stick, which lit-up the area.

Cheyenne was pleasantly surprised. "Where'd you get that?" she asked.

"I had 'em in my pack. Darren, gather your things."

Cheyenne moved back and once again felt something touch her ass. She turned and screamed when she realized it was the hand of a skeleton. Her fear quickly turned to embarrassment.

"Making new friends?" Nick asked with a smile. He looked at his watch—it was just after 11 AM—they had to hurry.

"Okay, listen—we've gotta move this rock," Nick said, moving into the smaller chamber. "See if you can find something to help roll it."

"Roll it?" Cheyenne asked.

"Yeah, we've gotta move it." He said commandingly. He pointed to where Darren stashed his gear, "There, grab the shovel and pickaxe."

They gathered around the large rock. Cheyenne and Darren wedged the pickaxe and shovel under it to get leverage to lift it up. Nick planted his feet against the wall nearest to the rock and rested his back against the boulder with his hands gripping its underside. This gave him leverage to push with his legs while lifting with his hands to get the large stone to move. He wished he had Jim and Speed here, but he didn't—he would have to make do without them.

"Okay everybody," Nick said, "On three...One... Two...Three."

They all gave a big groan as they pushed and pulled on the rock. Slowly, it began to move. Gradually, they were able to lift it up and start it slowly rolling.

“Be careful!” Nick groaned. “Don’t get under it!”

They didn’t understand why until the rock had finally rolled away, revealing an opening with another chamber below.

“You knew this was here?” Cheyenne asked, amazed.

Darren was still nervous about their situation, “What is it?” he asked.

“It’s our way out.” Nick said, smiling.

He dropped another glow-stick down the hole. The opening was about two feet wide, and two feet thick. Then it appeared to be about six or eight feet to the bottom below. They dropped their gear down first, and then each slid down through the opening.

After they were all down, Nick lit another stick. It was another large chamber. When the light of the glow sticks lit the room, Nick could hardly believe his eyes. There, in a neat large pile, was a stack of gold ingots. It looked like there were hundreds of them. He didn’t know what the value would be, but he knew it was more than he could imagine.

“Oh my God!” was all Cheyenne could say.

Nick looked over and saw Darren. He seemed to be too mesmerized to talk. It didn’t matter. They had a lot of work to do. This chamber was much larger than the one above them—and more like a large tunnel, with pools of water on the north and south ends. Nick felt around on the bottom of the side of the western wall. He felt moisture at an area that seemed to slope down from the rest of the chamber. That's where they needed to dig. Nick dropped a glow stick to mark the spot. Then he called to his nephew, who was still staring at the pile of gold bars. "Darren!"

"Yeah."

"See that area on the wall above the glow stick ?" Nick said, pointing to it.

"Yeah, I see it!"

"I want you to take that pick and open it up as much as you can."

"What?" Darren asked.

"Take your pick and open it up," Nick repeated. "That's our way out! Just be careful."

"Okay, Uncle Nick," Darren said enthusiastically, grabbing the pickaxe and making his way toward the light.

"Cheyenne!"

"Yeah?"

"Grab those bags out of the backpack and let's start loading these gold bars."

"I can do that," she said with a smile.

They loaded up the gold bars in sacks and moved them to where Darren was working, while Darren was successfully making a large opening to the outside. They filled up all the nylon bags they had and put more bars in their backpacks. There were still far more ingots left, but they would have to leave them. They would have to be happy with what they were able to carry out—it was still an amazing fortune in gold.

They finished loading the bags about the same time Darren finished digging out the opening. Since this was mostly soil, it was easier to dig out than the entrance had been. He was able to make it about three feet wide and about five feet tall—big enough to get them out.

Cheyenne went over to the opening and looked out. "Is this how we're getting out?" She asked with some doubt.

"Yeah," Nick said, walking over to the opening.

"It'll be a steep and difficult climb without any ropes—especially taking the gold," she said, looking down the side of the mountain.

"That's why it's good to have friends," Nick said looking out. He was relieved to see Jim and Speed on a small hill across from them. He pointed them out to Cheyenne and gave them a wave of acknowledgement. Jim saw his wave and waved back.

Jim and Speed were on their four-wheelers just waiting for a sign from their friends. When Jim saw them at the opening, he began to estimate the distance for his shot. When he saw Nick wave to him, he knew what that meant.

It was several hundred feet, and then he had to add in the height. He attached the thin cord to his arrow and planted his feet firmly. Taking a breath, he drew the bowstring back to his cheek. Raising his sight to the opening, he let the arrow fly.

"So, they weren't the cowards I thought they were!" Cheyenne said, amazed at the level of detail in Nick's plan. "What do we do next?"

"Well," Nick said confidently, turning around to her. "I give the signal, and then they'll send us a line."

As soon as he said it, he felt a whistling over his left shoulder. He was surprised to see the arrow whiz by him.

"Watch out!" Cheyenne yelled.

"What the hell!" Nick shouted with surprise. "I didn't give the signal!"

The arrow hit the wall just behind Nick's right shoulder and bounced off, landing on the cave floor. It was a perfect shot and the thin cord was still attached. They pulled in the thin cord—it was tied to a thicker climbing rope that would hold more weight. They tied the rope off in the cave to a boulder. Then they attached carabiners to the handles of the bags of gold and started sliding them down the line. Jim and Speed disconnected each bag as it arrived. They took out as much of the gold as they could. Then, after they got the gold out, Cheyenne made them shoulder harnesses and the three of them slid out too.

When Nick got across, he saw that they had four machines. They had somehow picked up Nick and Cheyenne's ATVs.

"Well?" Jim said, beaming with pride and looking at Nick.

"Yeah." Nick said. "Hell of a shot, Jimbo!"

"Who's your daddy now?" Jim asked sarcastically.

"Yeah well," Nick said. "You almost took my head off."

"I'll take that as a 'thank you'," Jim said to his friend. "See, Clutch comes through again."

"Yeah," Nick said and then looked over to the machines. "How'd you get these?"

"They came looking for us," Jim said nonchalantly.

"We didn't hurt 'em," Speed added, clicking his tongue. "We knocked 'em off the machines and took their guns. Pointed them south, and told 'em to get out of here."

"That's what I want you guys to do—but you need to head north," Nick said, looking at his watch. It was twelve o'clock noon. He started putting the sacks of gold bars on a steel box that was strapped on to the trailer. "You need to go—now!"

"Why?" Cheyenne asked. Just then, a large explosion went off about three hundred yards away.

"That's why!" Nick shouted. He reached into his pocket and pulled out Agent Diaz's card—he quickly handed it to Speed. "Get back to Sammy, have him call these guys and stop the artillery fire."

"What are you gonna do?" Speed asked, just as they heard another explosion.

"I'll be along shortly! Just get these guys out of here," Nick said with urgency in his voice.

"You got it!" Speed acknowledged, gunning his engine.

"Take 'em up past that little creek we crossed. You should be able to get phone reception there. Get 'em to safety!" Nick ordered.

"All right, let's go!" Jim yelled.

They got on their four-wheelers and roared off down the trail. They only had three machines, so Darren rode on back of Cheyenne's. Nick finished loading all the gold on the trailer and followed.

Even though his four-wheeler was larger, he was pulling a heavy trailer. The weight of the gold really slowed his machine down, so he wouldn't be able to go as fast. He knew this would be an issue, so he had a plan. And with a little time and a lot of luck, he might be able to pull it off.

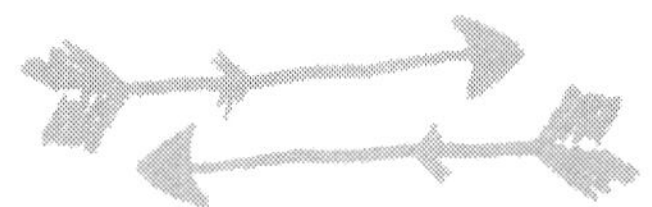

# Chapter 26
## War

Nick rode his four-wheeler hard, but with the heavy weight of the trailer and chest of gold he couldn't keep up—losing sight of his friends. When he got to the creek, he stopped and looked around. Then he rode along its bank until he found the right spot. To his left, he saw a bend in the creek, about two hundred feet away—the water looked to be deeper at that part. Spotting a tree across from the creek bend, it looked to be a perfect spot for what he had in mind.

The creek was about a foot deep, so he drove his ATV in the water to the bend—he made sure not to drive in too deep. The water only came up to the four-wheeler's tires. Across from the bend, he got off his machine and tightly tied up the chest of gold with a long rope. Then he shoved it off the back of the small trailer. He had positioned the trailer so that the chest slid off into the deepest part of the creek. However, the creek bed was so shallow it barely covered the chest—this was the best he could do. He then took the rope and ran it across the creek, tying it securely to the tree on the bank. He also took mental note of the surrounding hills and terrain so he could come back later and find it again.

When Diego left the camp with the golden cross, he drove off on a four-wheeler. He thought it would be faster and he left his men to drive the SUVs because these would be slower and harder to maneuver on the rocky trail. However, just about the time he made it to the other side of the mountain, the engine started sputtering and the four-wheeler came to a halt. It took Diego some time to realize it was out of gas.

Artillery rounds were starting to explode all over the area. The blasts were making the ground shake and rocks sprayed from each explosion. He needed to get out of there quickly with the gold cross.

Fortunately, there was a can of gasoline strapped on the back, but it still took him precious time to refuel. As soon as he was done, he started back on the trail. Eventually, he came across a small creek. Crossing it, he saw something from the corner of his eye. Suddenly, he recognized Nick and he froze. He couldn't believe his eyes.

"Am I looking at a man or a ghost?" Diego asked Nick, in amazement, as he quickly turned his ATV and rode up closer to him. "I left you for dead in that cave! How—"

"Oh, I'm human." Nick cut him off. "More or less."

"But… but you escaped," Diego said astonished, as he drove his machine up to Nick's.

"And you survived." Nick nodded towards the open desert as the blasts continued not far from them.

Diego was dumbfounded. "But how?" He asked, getting off his ATV and standing in the shallow part of the creek bed. "A secret tunnel perhaps?"

"I got some help." Nick quipped as he noticed the dark clouds and torrential rain that was quickly moving towards them. Diego was now standing in between the two ATVs, just off to Nick's left.

Diego looked Nick up and down, trying to guess how he might have escaped the sealed cave. "Your spirit friends maybe helped you, huh?" Diego speculated, while pulling out his pistol. He looked at the rope in Nick's hand and followed it out to the deep part of the creek.

"Maybe."

"Well, I'm sorry my friend," Diego said, realizing Nick was hiding something. "But I don't think those spirits can help you now. It looks like they intend for me to have the treasure."

Nick looked down at the rope in his hand and realized that Diego knew exactly what it was tied to. "Don't guess you'd consider sharing." He watched Diego grin and slowly shake his head 'no'. "Yeah, I didn't think so."

"You should have stayed in the cave, my friend." Diego then raised his pistol with his right hand, pointing it at Nick. "Now, drop the rope and back up to that tree."

Just at that moment there was a rumbling coming from behind him—the sound was getting louder and louder. Instead of letting the rope go, Nick twirled his hand around it, lashing it to his wrist and gripping it tightly. At first Diego thought he was being defiant and cocked his pistol. But then, he noticed the strange look on Nick's face, who was looking past him.

Diego looked over his shoulder then turned around in time to see a wall of water and mud coming at him. He had heard of flash floods, but he had never been in the path of one. He froze in the face of the oncoming water and debris that was moving at a rapid speed.

The wall of water and mud hit them with such force that it crashed one of the four-wheelers into the other—with Diego smashed in between. The two ends of the rope were both securely tied to the tree and chest, which was so heavy as to act like an anchor.

Diego's ATV was tumbling by Nick, so he reached out with his left hand and just barely caught the canvas bag with the golden cross. He quickly pulled the strap of the bag over his shoulder. He held on for dear life to the rope with both hands as the pressure of the water was growing more difficult to fight against. Holding on to the rope and bag, he fought the current to lift his left leg over the rope, hooking his knee around it to keep from being washed away.

Just then a larger surge of the flood knocked him underwater. The pressure of the water was almost impossible to fight against, as the creek swelled to a formidable six feet deep now and was flowing extremely fast. Nick pulled himself along on the rope, positioning himself behind a large boulder, which allowed the water and debris to flow around and past him.

When Nick was finally able to raise his head out of the water, he saw the two four-wheelers floating down the creek. He also saw Diego's lifeless body floating face down. The large boulder had greatly reduced the force of the flash flood on him. He was lucky to be alive.

Further up the trail, Cheyenne and the others had met at the rendezvous point and were waiting for Nick. There were also other men who had shown up—some government-types in suits—who seemed totally out of place out here. Mostly they were talking to Sammy, but Cheyenne's concern was for Nick. She was worried that he hadn't made it out safely. Maybe she should go back to find him.

Speed and Jim could see the worried look on her face and they looked at each other with looks of questioning whether they should go back for him as well.

Cheyenne was just about to climb on an ATV when she saw a dark figure that appeared just over the hill—carrying something and plodding along the gravel road. She wasn't sure who it was at first but as he drew nearer she could make out the features of his face. He was smiling and she knew it was him—She was relieved to see Nick's large silhouette coming into full view now.

There was no sign of his four-wheeler or the gold chest. And as he approached, everyone could see that he was wet and carrying a canvas bag. His whole team cheered and was ecstatic to see that he made it out alive.

Hansen, the big blonde DEA agent, walked up first to meet him. "So, did you find anything?" he asked, with a big grin on his face.

"Yeah, I found something." Nick snickered as he walked up to him. With the bag in his left hand, he quickly delivered a powerful reverse punch with his right hand, into Hansen's solar plexus. Hansen doubled over in pain, his whole body paralyzed, as Nick walked past him. Agents Goldberg and Diaz looked on without saying a word.

Nick looked at agent Diaz and pointed over his shoulder with his thumb. "If you're still looking for Diego, his body's floating west, down the next wash."

"Oh Nick!" Cheyenne cried, rushing up to him and giving him a big hug, "I'm so glad…" Suddenly realizing she might be displaying inappropriate affection, she pulled back and tried to contain her excitement. "I'm… I'm glad you're alive."

"You are?" Nick asked, his arms still around her waist.

"Yes," she said smiling, thinking the answer was obvious.

He looked at her and smiled. "I'm kind of happy about that too."

They looked in each other's eyes and he didn't let go of her until the others came over. They were all slapping him on the back and giving him high fives.

"What happened?" Jim asked.

Sammy jumped in, "Yeah, what the hell happened back there?"

“I had a little problem,” Nick lowered the canvas bag off his shoulder and flung it to Sammy. “But I was able to save that,” he said smiling.

Sammy quickly opened the bag and pulled out the golden cross. He broke into a huge smile, looking at the valuable artifact.

“Yeah!” Sammy hollered as he lifted the cross over his head, showing it off to the others. They all celebrated with “Oohs” and “Aahs” as they passed it around.

A smile even came to Goldberg’s face. Of course, he was calculating in his mind what the government’s cut would be.

Nick remained standing next to Cheyenne. His eyes returned back to hers—his heart filled with emotions. He knew he was taking a chance, but he no longer cared. He tightened his grip on her waist with both hands and pulled her body up against his. Cheyenne could feel the dampness of his shirt, but offered no resistance. Leaning his head down, he covered her lips with his—kissing her passionately. She surrendered to him completely. Lost in the moment, they were both oblivious to the stares they were now getting from the others.

# Chapter 27

## Spirit Redemption

A couple of days later, Nick drove his car down North Central Avenue with Cheyenne. All he had told her was that he needed to meet with someone. So, he pulled into a parking lot and waited until he saw the old man come out of the church across the street—evening Mass must have just ended.

"Wait here," he said to her, as he opened the car door. "I won't be long."

"Where are you going?" she asked.

"I told you, I need to talk to someone. Stay here, I'll be right back."

It was the same place where he first caught up with the old man, walking towards the restaurant. Most people are creatures of habit—even priests. However, this time there were two young men walking with him—they were in regular street clothes and weren't wearing a priest's collar or vestments. One was tall and lean the other was shorter and stocky. Maybe Father Martin was taking precautions and hired bodyguards. Their presence made Nick wonder just what agent Goldberg had told him.

"Father Martin!" Nick called out, coming up behind them.

The old priest looked rather startled when he looked back and saw that it was Nick calling him. He looked back and forth at the young men and then nodded to the one closest to Nick.

"I just want to talk." Nick said, trying to put them at ease.

"I don't think so." The stocky one said, as he walked toward Nick in a forceful manner.

He then moved in front of Nick, blocking his path to the old priest. When he moved in even closer, Nick made his move. Taking his left hand, he grabbed the man's right shoulder while also grabbing the man's left shoulder, then spun him around while moving in behind him. Once Nick was at his back, he grabbed his left arm and twisted it behind him while hooking his right hand around the man's throat. The whole thing happened in the blink of an eye. Now Nick was holding the man in between himself and the taller one.

Nick held the man easily as he continued to struggle. The second, taller man, unsure of what to do, put his hand inside his jacket.

"I wouldn't do that," Nick said, thinking he may have a weapon.

The tall man looked over at Father Martin, who was shaking his head 'no'. The man then pulled his hand out holding it up, empty of any weapons.

The man Nick was holding continued to flail around until Nick tightened his choke around the man's neck, putting pressure to his carotid arteries. In a matter of seconds, the man went limp and passed out. Nick then pushed him into the arms of the taller man. Whoever these guys were, they weren't trained very well. Maybe that's what you get when you use altar boys for your security, Nick thought.

"Father," Nick said, pointing to the side of the building. "Let's go for a walk."

The old priest was shaken by Nick's ability to over take his men so easily. This made him readily compliant with Nick's request. Nick then put his hand on the shoulder of the priest and led him away. They left the two bodyguards there, the taller one trying to revive the stocky one, as they walked around to the side of the building. When they were out of everyone's sight, Nick stopped.

"So, Father," Nick began. "When we talked earlier, you knew what Father Neve had done, didn't you?"

Father Martin looked around nervously and wiped his brow, "What do you mean?"

"I mean the dead bodies," Nick said. "What did he do? Did he write about it in his journals?"

Father Martin could see the anger in Nick's eyes and realized he was cornered. "Uh… well, he…he alluded to it," the old priest confessed.

"What did he and the other Jesuits do? Huh?" Nick asked. "They took away the Indian's religion and converted them to Christianity. Then they convinced them that it was 'God's will' to mine the gold for them,—am I right?"

The priest looked down shamefully and admitted, "Yes, yes."

"And when it got time to leave, they rounded up those that knew where the gold was, gathered them all in that cave, and sealed it up—burying those poor souls alive—just to keep their secret hidden. Didn't they?"

Father Martin could no longer hold in this dark secret and he finally broke down. "Okay!" he conceded. "Yes… he did it! Father Neve—before he was arrested with the others."

Nick was surprised at the quick admission of the old priest, but this only created more questions. "And you, Father Martin—what's *your* role?" He asked. "You go around, making sure no one finds out the truth—so you can keep the church's reputation intact? Is that it? Did you tell Diego that we were going out there?"

"No, but I suspected that you might," Father Martin admitted. "You don't seem like a man who gives up easily."

"I don't," Nick said with conviction.

Father Martin paused in deep thought then looked Nick in the eyes with solemnity. "Well, If it's any consolation," he said. "Father Neve regretted what he did for the rest of his life. He spent his last days in penance and praying for forgiveness."

Nick raised his eyebrows and nodded in acknowledgement. "He did?"

"Yes, he did!" The old priest said with further conviction.

Nick's face looked sympathetically at the priest—and then quickly turned to anger. "Sorry Father, but that's not good enough," Nick snapped. "It's time people were told the truth about what happened out there."

Taken aback at Nick's change of demeanor he asked, "And how will you do that?"

Nick grinned and said, "With this," as he pulled a small tape recorder out of his pants pocket. He held it up to show that he had been recording their conversation. "And I've got photographs too."

"photographs?"

"Yes!" Nick said confidently. "I got inside the cave—and I took photos of the skeletons buried inside there."

"Huh!" Father Martin scoffed.

"Yeah, I got proof." Nick affirmed.

"Proof?" Father Martin sneered.

Nick could see the old man was acting dubious. "That's right!" He insisted.

"No," the old priest disagreed, slowly shaking his head. "I'm afraid that all you have is the ramblings of an old man." He said in an almost whispering tone.

"And the pictures?" Nick asked, feeling he had the old man trapped.

"What? Pictures of skeleton bones—in a dimly lit cave?" the priest said dismissively. "Those could have come from anywhere."

Nick looked the old man up and down, realizing that he was probably right. There wasn't anything in the pictures to show where they had been taken—nothing to show even *when* they were taken. Beside, he knew the old priest had years of practice in discrediting people. "You son of a bitch," Nick growled at him.

"I am sorry about what happened to those people," Father Martin said in a sympathetic tone. "But, we gave them a purpose to their lives—a meaning to their existence."

That was enough to set Nick off the edge. He grabbed the priest by the throat and pushed him up against the wall of the building. Holding him with his left hand, he held his right hand back with a clenched fist.

"What are you going to do now?" Father Martin taunted, struggling to keep his glasses on. "Kill me?"

"I should," Nick snarled. "As far as I'm concerned, you're just as guilty as they are—you're an accomplice. But, I'm not going to kill you."

Expecting the worse, the priest was surprised. "You're not?"

"No," Nick said, looking at the scared, old man in front of him. "I'm going to do the same thing to you that you did to those Indians."

"I…I don't understand."

Nick whispered forcefully. "I'm going to give *your* life purpose."

The priest was completely confused now. "Huh?"

"Now," Nick said, with a diabolical grin. "You can spend the rest of *your* days in penance and prayer—wondering what kind of special place in Hell, God has planned for you."

Nick's words sank in to the priest like a tragic revelation—his eyes grew dim and his face turned white. Nick knew by the expression on his face, that he had struck a nerve. Even at this stage of his life, the old 'man of faith' had to admit to himself that he had sealed his own fate.

As Nick let go of him, the priest's body went limp and he slowly slumped down the wall in shame. Nick left him like that as he turned away—walking back around to the parking lot.

Seeing Nick come from the side of the building, the two young men ran past him to attend to the old priest.

Cheyenne was still in the car waiting, when he returned. She had seen what had happened with the men in the parking lot. Then she watched as Nick walked around the corner with the priest. Her curiosity was killing her.

"What happened?" She said anxiously, as he got back in the car.

"Huh?" Nick said casually, as he started the engine.

"What was with those guys?" Cheyenne asked, having seen the altercation.

"Oh," Nick minimized. "Just a misunderstanding."

"A misunderstanding?" She said with doubt. "And what about that other guy—the priest?" Cheyenne was excited to hear all about it, but Nick seemed completely unfazed by the whole thing—almost like it had never happened.

"Who? The priest?" Nick said, feigning ignorance.

"Yes!" Cheyenne said impatiently. "What did he have to say?"

"Oh," he said, looking over at her. "He said he was 'sorry'."

"Sorry?" She repeated. Now she was getting frustrated and said "Nick if this is going to work between us, you need to talk to me. Tell me what you're feeling, what you're thinking."

"You're right," Nick nodded his head in agreement. "Right now, I'm feeling hungry—and I'm thinking Chinese sounds real good."

Cheyenne rolled her eyes in disappointment, and shook her head. 'What the hell just happened?', she wondered. She was anxious to learn more, but Nick wasn't offering anything else. Only making jokes about her curiosity. And for that, she slapped him on the arm to make sure he knew she was unhappy with him.

Nick wanted to tell her everything. The whole thing had made him very angry. However, he knew how sensitive she could be. And he wasn't sure if he wanted to burden her with what he had learned about the Jesuits and the murder of the Indian people. He also wasn't sure what good it would do to tell her anyway. Maybe he would try to explain everything later on.

So for now, Nick just calmly drove out of the parking lot and onto the main road while Cheyenne sat quietly next to him. She could only hope that he would eventually explain all of this to her in his own time.

# Chapter 28
## Answers

Later that night, Nick and the others sat at a table in the bar. Everyone was there except Sammy and Darren,—both of them had left town. Darren was back in Alaska getting ready for college. That was part of their deal. Sammy had gone back to Florida. He was setting up meetings with appraisers for the gold cross.

There was a decent crowd at 'Rockers' for a Thursday night. Rock music from the jukebox was playing in the background. They had ordered a round of drinks and were toasting to a successful hunt. This was their first chance to discuss everything that had happened—and Nick knew they had a lot of questions. He had asked them all to be patient and give him a little time. He wanted to wait until he could get them all together—that way he wouldn't have to constantly repeat himself.

As hard as it was for them, they all agreed. Even Cheyenne, but now with everyone gathered, she knew he would have to give her some straight answers.

"So, how did you know that we'd be able to get out of the cave and off the mountain?" she asked, sipping her soda.

Nick looked at Jim and Speed, nodding, and then back to her. "George Rogers showed me and Jim what he thought the layout of the mountain was. He thought there was water running thru the second chamber most of the year, and that they had drained it out to make it usable. He did a lot of research on this and I counted on him being right," Nick continued. "I knew that if I could find the entrance, they would have to keep us alive to dig it out. That's why it was important that Jim and Speed not get caught. They had to be able to get us out of there."

Cheyenne furrowed her brow. "So, how did you know they wouldn't kill us?"

Nick took a swig of his beer and replied, "Well, I wasn't certain, but I knew Diego wouldn't do his own dirty work. That's why I did my best to thin out the number of his men. Besides, they didn't really need to kill us—they just needed to leave us behind. Diego thought for certain he had left us for dead. You should have seen the look on his face when he saw me at that creek."

Nick shook his head and chuckled, remembering the look on Diego's face. The others laughed too, trying to imagine it.

Jim added, "That was just before the flash flood, right?"

"Yeah," Nick said, getting serious again as he remembered the events. "I hadn't really counted on that—it was pure luck that I made it out of there."

Jim raised his bottle and said, "Here's to luck," and they all clinked their drinks together.

Speed finally asked the one thing that was on everyone's mind, "And what about the chest?"

"Not to worry, it's well hidden," Nick reassured. "As soon as the army training quiets down, I'll go back out there and get it. But, the other thing about the gold..."

"What?" Jim asked excitedly.

Nick held his hand up with his palm out. "Remember what George said? We want to convert it to cash slowly. I can't just show up somewhere with a ton of gold bars."

"You're right," Jim nodded in agreement.

Speed took a drink of his beer and said, "Yeah, you don't want people asking too many questions."

"I'm gonna do it slowly and methodically," Nick said. "Don't worry, everyone will get their share."

"Does Sammy know about the chest?" Cheyenne asked.

"No. He's busy getting appraisals on that cross. Don't worry about him, that gold cross will more than cover all the expenses he paid out and then some. It should bring in quite a bit at auction."

"Are you ever gonna tell him about the chest?" Jim asked.

Nick grinned, "Maybe. But, I'm gonna let him sweat it out first. I still wanna know how Diego knew we'd be back out there."

Always thinking the best of people, Cheyenne suggested, "Maybe Diego just got lucky?"

Nick knew Sammy better than her, but decided to remain open to this possibility. "Maybe," he shrugged, taking another swig of his beer.

"And the Feds? Who called them?" She asked.

"Agent Diaz told me that they had pieced it together after finding out that the land was going back to the Army."

A waitress came over, taking their empty bottles and they ordered another round from her.

The conversation was lagging when Cheyenne spoke up. "Have you told them what we've decided to do?" She looked at the group and then back at Nick.

Speed wrinkled his brow. "About what?" he asked. The whole idea of Nick and Cheyenne planning something without the others made him wonder if they were about to announce something of a personal nature. "What do you two have going on now?"

"It's about our share of the treasure," Cheyenne said, looking at Speed and Jim.

Any mention of something happening to the treasure made them a bit nervous. "What about the treasure?" Jim asked, looking sternly at Nick.

Nick looked at Cheyenne and nodded that she should tell them.

"We're going to give most of it back to the Indian people," she announced.

"What?" Jim cocked his head at Nick. "After what we all went through—what *you* went through?"

Nick raised his eyebrows and smiled—lifting his beer. "Yeah," he said, nodding.

"That's...that's crazy!" Speed sputtered.

"Yeah," Jim said, tilting his beer towards Speed "What he said."

Cheyenne caressed Nick's bicep in a show of support. "We think it's the right thing to do," she said firmly.

Nick nodded his head in agreement then added, "They gave their lives for it. It's just the right thing to do." He raised his beer in a toast and said, "May they always be remembered!"

They all raised their bottles and clinked in respect for the dead. That's when they heard a voice from behind Nick.

"Hey Asshole!"

"Uh-oh," Jim mumbled, looking back over Nick's shoulder. "What do we got here?"

Nick looked around the table at his friends. They were all looking at someone behind him.

"How many of them are there?" Nick whispered to Jim.

Jim whispered out of the corner of his mouth, "Two—maybe three."

"You guys got my back?" Nick said in a low tone, expecting complete support.

"You know me." Jim said, raising his hands. "I'm a lover."

Speed raised his bottle, winked and clicked his tongue. "I got faith in ya."

"Thanks!" Nick said sarcastically.

Cheyenne looked at Jim and Speed with contempt and said, "You two are real chicken shits—you know that?"

"Hey, I'm talking to you!" the voice boomed behind him.

Nick took a swig of his beer and put it quietly down on the table. He casually turned around in his chair and slowly stood up. The were two men, about ten feet away. One was about six foot two with long brown hair—maybe in his mid-twenties. The other one Nick recognized as the one he had gotten into a fight with before. This new one must be his brother.

"What's the problem?" Nick asked.

"My brother told me what you said—about we should move to another town."

"Oh yeah, I remember now." Nick said, smiling. "Your brother told me that you two were the toughest guys in your town—and I told him, 'you need to move to a bigger town.'"

Upon hearing that, people started to gather around and began to laugh. This made the man angry.

"That's right, funny man."

"And now you want to know if I can help you move?" Nick quipped. "Sorry, but I'm really busy this weekend."

Again, people started laughing. The man couldn't let this guy make a fool of him and his brother. They had a reputation to live up to.

"That's it asshole!" the man yelled. He charged Nick and threw a punch with his right hand.

Nick easily deflected the punch and pushed the man off balance, right toward Jim. Jim quickly stood up and guided him directly into a table of patrons next to them, knocking a couple of them down. This led to one of them getting up and sucker punching Jim in the jaw. A chain reaction ensued where Speed got up and punched the guy that hit Jim. The entire scene quickly escalated into a full on bar brawl.

Cheyenne watched in amazement as it all unfolded—smiling and shaking her head as if disappointed, but thoroughly entertained. Nick was unlike anyone she knew—the element of danger that seemed to surround him, certainly brought excitement into her world. She looked back at Nick just in time to see someone coming up to him from behind.

"Nick, look out!" She yelled.

Nick turned quickly to see the other brother swinging a beer bottle at his head. He blocked the bottle with his right hand and punched him in the jaw with his left...